There I Find Hope

Strawberry Sands Book Six

Jessie Gussman

Published By: Jessie Gussman

Contents

Acknowledgments

Cover art by Kim Killion of The Killion Group
Editing by Heather Hayden
Narration by Jay Dyess
Author Services by CE Author Assistant

Listen to the unabridged audio for FREE performed by Jay Dyess on the Say with Jay channel on YouTube. Get early access to all of Jay's recordings and listen to Jessie's books before they're available to the general public, plus get daily Bible readings by Jay and bonus scenes by becoming a Say with Jay channel member.

Chapter 1

The scent of rotting flowers made Sunday Landry want to puke.

The flowers weren't really rotting, but the smell made her sick nonetheless. For the rest of her life, she would hate the smell of flowers because she would associate it with the funeral of her son.

She wiped her cheek and listened to the lady in front of her as she spoke about growing up in Strawberry Sands and how she had not talked to Sunday since she was a child and how sad she was that Blake had drowned.

Sunday listened. Truly she did. Or at least she tried to. But she didn't really hear anything. It felt like a hundred people screamed inside of her head, arguing, fighting, although she didn't know over what, all she knew was that she could hardly stand it, and she wanted to get away.

Except, one could hardly run out of the funeral of one's son.

Plus, she hadn't quite gotten used to the idea that her son didn't need her anymore. There was the idea in her head that she needed to stay, to take care of him, that he needed her. Responsible mothers didn't just walk out on their kid without taking him with her or making sure he was cared for.

But her son lay stiff and cold in the casket, and it was all her fault.

Why had she decided to go on a walk on the beach?

Why had she stood admiring the horses and allowed her gaze to track off her son for even one second?

It wasn't like she had spent three hours not paying any attention to her son at all.

Blake had known better. He'd grown up around Lake Michigan. He knew he couldn't just run into the water without a life vest and without his mother's permission.

But he'd been chasing a ball. A huge, rogue wave had knocked him down. Sunday had turned around in time to see that.

She called to him immediately, started running right away, but her feet sank into the sand and it felt like she ran in slow motion. That was what her night-mare had been every night since. Run-ning in slow motion.

She kept running and running and couldn't go any faster. Couldn't reach the water in time. And when she did get there, she couldn't find him.

The waves had been high, the riptide strong, and while she knew she would have jumped in the lake to save him, she couldn't see him.

She had her phone out of her pocket dialing 911 as she ran and was mostly incoherent as she spoke on the phone.

They sent people anyway, divers, men with boats, someone even showed up with a dog. An ambulance had sat on the beach, its lights flashing, like there was some hope that they would fish her son out of the water and he would still be alive and they would rush him off to the hospital and he would survive.

Even as she prayed for that to happen, she knew it was impossible. Although God was a God of miracles, wasn't He?

Apparently she didn't qualify for miracles.

She hardly ever asked for anything. She asked for one little thing—the life of her son—and God did not grant her wish. Her desire. Her one longing.

She didn't even ask for her marriage to be reconciled. She hadn't asked for it to be saved. She hadn't even asked God why her husband had cheated, after he'd spent the years they'd been married neglecting her and spending time on his hobbies and online rather than with her.

She just asked for the life of her son.

And God said no.

She supposed she felt the way a child usually felt when they wanted something with all their heart and their parent turned them down.

She felt a little angry, a little put out. Annoyed. Heartbroken. Was there something worse than being heartbroken? If there was, Sunday was that thing that was worse. The very worst thing that anyone could become was what she was right now.

How did one survive, let alone get over, the death of their child?

Why had she walked on the beach that day? Why had she taken her eyes off her kid? Why hadn't she made him hold her hand?

She knew why. She lived here. She'd grown up here. Lake Michigan was something she respected, yes, but not a scary thing. And she thought she'd trained her son to obey. To listen. To respect the lake just as she did.

"You know this is just one of those fluke things that happen. Something you couldn't have stopped. Something you couldn't have changed. It's just God's will."

Really? Was God's will for her to lose her child?

She looked at the lady who was patting her arm. She recognized her as someone she'd grown up with. Gone to church with. Known all of her life. She wanted to grab her by the throat and pin her on the floor and tell her that God didn't will for her son to die.

It was her fault. She was the world's worst mother. She didn't deserve to be a mother. Blake should have had some-one better.

She didn't manage to smile, but she nod-ded and wiped the tear that trickled out of her eye.

She couldn't go back to her apartment above the candy store. There were too many reminders of her son there. His toys, his clothes, a load of his laundry was still in the dryer. Tuesday had been a nice day, and she decided that she and Blake would go for a walk instead.

He begged to take his ball, and she con-sented without really thinking about it. It would give him something to do as she walked up the beach, thinking about life and things and giving herself a break from the struggle of trying to make her business profitable.

Thankfully her mom paid her for cleaning the rooms at the bed-and-breakfast, or she would have gone under three years ago when she moved to Strawberry Sands after her divorce.

Strawberry Sands was growing, getting bigger every year, more popular with the tourists, and she had high hopes for her candy store.

But now? She never wanted to set foot in her apartment again. Someone else could handle cleaning it out, except she couldn't stand the thought of that either. Couldn't stand the thought of every memory of her son being wiped out. His toys gone. His clothes gone. His presence gone from her life.

She turned back to the well-wishers and tried to focus on their words.

Then, the only thing that could have made her day any worse happened.

Her ex walked in.

Glenn's new wife held tight to his hand while her son from her first marriage held her other hand.

Sunday recognized them easily. She'd seen them multiple times. During and after the divorce.

Apparently Diana ran around with Glenn for a while before Sunday figured it all out. Up until that point, Sunday had been trying to work on her marriage. To get in shape after having a child so her husband would find her attractive. To cook his favorite meals and spend time rubbing his back and feet, asking him questions about his day and listening as he spoke. Sending him sexy texts and buying new lingerie. Reading tons of articles with titles like "what men like in the bedroom," studying them, and putting every idea possible in practice.

Of course, once she found out about Diana, she figured out exactly why Glenn was no longer interested in Sunday.

Diana was everything Sunday wasn't. Slender, with the body of a ballerina, flexible and supple. She was actually an inch or so taller than Glenn, willowy, thin, graceful, and she could probably twist herself into all the pretzels that the articles recommended.

Sunday, on the other hand, still carried around the extra baby weight she had before she even had a baby. She had wide hips from her father's side of the family and no bust.

She was a pear with an apple belly.

Not that any of that mattered now. It wouldn't bring Blake back.

Glenn didn't stop at the back. He moved forward with confidence, walking up the aisle.

She talked to him on the phone, although by the time she was able to call him, there was nothing he could do. And with Glenn being a practical man, analytical and data driven, he didn't bother to make the drive to Strawberry Sands. After all, if Blake was dead, there was nothing for him to come to.

Except the funeral, apparently.

Sunday had sent him the details but hadn't expected him to attend. They'd shared custody, with Glenn seeming to be happy with two weeks with Blake in the summer, and two weeks over Christmas, and an occasional weekend throughout the year.

Probably Diana was happy with that.

Sunday couldn't imagine only seeing her son for four weeks and a few days every year.

Her world revolved around her son. Him and the candy shop.

Glenn didn't bother to wait in line; he walked around the folks who were standing, which was pretty much everyone in Strawberry Sands who hadn't already shaken Sunday's hand or hugged her, and he pushed in front of the person who was next without bothering to say "excuse me."

"Mother of the year. Right here," he said.

Yeah, she didn't expect sympathy from him. He wasn't exactly a compassionate person. He was the data analysist for some bigwig company in Chicago, and facts were all that mattered to him.

"Glenn. Everyone says it was an accident. Don't be so hard on her," Diana said beside him, her voice as smooth as chocolate, even if her look was a little condescending. Maybe that was Sunday's imagination, since she had to look up to her. With her tall, willowy figure and her long blonde hair, gorgeous blue eyes, and features that looked like they were lifted directly from an airbrushed magazine, she could have been a model.

Still, any kind of compassion was a lifeline especially after Glenn's few words. He didn't need to say much in order to hurt her already aching heart.

Sunday swallowed. The lessons from her childhood came to the forefront; they'd become automatic over the years, her default. Thankfully.

"I put his favorite outfit on him. He's wearing his favorite sneakers. I know he can't take his toys with him, but I put a few of his favorites in the casket." Her voice, already soft, broke on the last few words.

She turned her head, unable to look directly at the still form of her son but letting her eyes drift to the corner of the coffin. Casket. Casket was a much better word. Coffin sounded so...dead.

She swallowed again. Her throat tight, sore from crying and from trying not to cry, and from being unable to stop crying, maybe from a little screaming as well.

No one ever said that when one loses a child, crying takes over one's life. The thought of it, doing it, trying not to do it, recovering from doing it, thinking about doing it again.

It was all there. All in her heart. The crying. Everything.

Glenn lifted his chin, acknowledging her words while at the same time making sure she understood she wasn't on his level. She was beneath him.

The child beside Diana fussed a little, tugging at his mom's hand, holding onto it, leaning down.

"Be still," she said, and the words sounded harsh to Sunday.

Sunday wanted to tell her that she needed to be kind. To appreciate the little tug on her arm, the squirming child beside her, not to worry about whether he was inconveniencing her or not, because the day might come when she didn't have to worry about him moving. She didn't have to worry about him wanting to do something other than what he was supposed to do. When he would be gone forever.

"He doesn't have his red truck. That was his favorite." Glenn leaned over the casket and looked at it dispassionately, like the kid that was lying there so still was not his. "Of course, if you were actually a mother who cared about him, you would have known what his favorite color was."

Glenn's words hurt. She already felt like she was a terrible mom, and while she knew that Blake's favorite color was blue, and Glenn obviously didn't have a clue, was just saying things designed to put her down and hurt her, his words just confirmed her thought that she was a terrible mom.

"But being with you all the time, he was turning into a bit of a sissy. Last time he was in my house, he wanted to play with one of Breanna's dolls. I wasn't going to let that happen." Glenn gave a humorless laugh, which Sunday barely heard.

It was one thing for him to insult her. She deserved it. It was another thing for him to say something so unkind about her son.

After she recovered, she would realize that there really wasn't anything that terrible about what he said, but maybe it was the grief, maybe it was her lack of sleep, maybe it was just the fact that she had lost her only child and she was completely devastated, but his words made red fill up her vision until a rage burst in her chest, until the default actions of her childhood were totally obliterated and the only thing she could think of was to hurt the man who had caused so much pain in her son's life.

"You are a—" and a word, profane and vile, came out of her mouth. It was a word she had never said before in her life, but it rolled off her tongue like she'd said it since babyhood, smooth and fitting and so very, very satisfying.

But that wasn't the most amazing thing that happened. At least, hearing the story told later, the most amazing thing was that her fingers curled into claws, her face twisted in outrage, and her body lunged at her ex-husband, knocking Diana and Sidney down in the process.

Chapter 2

Noah stood uncomfortably at the back of the church. He really didn't belong here. Except, he was a resident of Strawberry Sands and had gone to school with Sunday Landry.

He had a huge crush on her too. At one point, they'd been good friends. He had hoped for more, but she'd been swept off her feet by the man she eventually married when they were seniors in high school and he'd come to do a presentation about careers.

Noah wasn't sure of the details, because once Sunday had met Glenn, she hadn't had much time for him.

And that was understandable. He had more than one friend who had fallen in love and had neglected their regular friends for a while until the newness of their infatuation wore off.

But Sunday had married and moved away and Noah had gone off to college, and they had never reconnected. Even though she rented her candy store from his company which owned the building.

He didn't think she knew that. It wasn't common knowledge in town. He didn't go around announcing to everyone that his business had been successful, or that he'd come back to Strawberry Sands and invested in the town he loved and grew up in.

He'd been biding his time since Sunday moved back. Several large projects had taken his time in Chicago. One—a hotel just north of Strawberry Sands—had just been approved and they were breaking ground on it soon.

But this... He couldn't even fathom the pain she must be going through now. Because he cared for her—high school was a long time ago, but he supposed he was the kind of man who was friends forever—he wanted to do something, anything, to help her. But he didn't know what. So he just showed up at the funeral. His heart aching, his soul longing to help, his hands itching to do something. But all he could do was stand in the back, awkward, nodding to the people he knew, which was almost everyone, and wondering if Sunday really wanted him to come up and give his condolences. Or if she'd prefer to not have to interact with almost strangers.

He decided that he would simply go to the casket, stand respectfully in front of it for a few moments, and then walk out, not adding to the line of greeters and hence the amount of time Sunday had to spend on her feet.

Seeing him might dig up memories she would rather keep buried. Not that they had any bad blood between them, it was just he was around when she decided to run off with Glenn, which had obviously not worked out well for her.

As Noah stopped in front of the casket, he glanced over and narrowed his eyes. The man standing in front of her now, holding tightly to the hand of a slender blonde woman, who gripped the hand of a young child, looked a lot like an older version of what he remembered Glenn to look like.

The man spoke to Sunday, whose grief-laden face suddenly looked stricken, like the man had stabbed her in the heart.

Noah's jaw tightened, but if that was Glenn, Noah knew divorces could be nasty, and perhaps Sunday was still in love with him. Obviously, he had moved on.

Noah turned his face back toward the casket, not really wanting to look at the lifeless little boy, the one he'd seen cheerfully holding onto Sunday's hand, skipping up and down the sidewalk, his laughter ringing out over the streets as Sunday's smile lit up her entire face.

He had several memories like that, times when he'd seen Sunday looking so happy that he'd almost approached her.

Perhaps it was just fear, but he didn't want to approach her and be rebuffed, because that felt like it was a final thing. He'd spent so much of his time thinking about Sunday and wanting to be with her that if he had been rejected, he wasn't sure exactly what he would do. He didn't want to face the reality that Sunday would never be his.

He'd just started to move away from the casket when sudden movement out of the corner of his eye made him freeze, and then a woman screaming profanity made him turn.

The woman was Sunday.

In all the time he had known her, Noah had never known her to say anything inappropriate, let alone allow the words that were erupting out of her mouth to see the light of day. There was no doubt of what she was saying. But the even more shocking thing was that she had launched herself at Glenn, her hands curled like eagle's talons, as she swiped at his face and neck. He lifted his hands, trying to ward her off while the force of her efforts made him backpedal. He retreated right into the front pew, where he plopped down, with Sunday on top of him.

That was all it took for Noah to launch himself toward the fighting couple. A portion of his mind realized that the graceful woman who had been with Glenn was now on the ground along with her child who had started to cry, but she wasn't the woman he was concerned about.

It seemed like the entire population of the church converged on the front pew, but since Noah had been so close, he was the first to arrive.

He grabbed Sunday by the waist and pulled her back, assuming that if Glenn was able to right himself, he would not attack her back, if the man was indeed Glenn.

"Let me go! How dare you insult my son! Especially when you were such a pathetic father who never gave a flip about anything!" Sunday struggled, continuing to hurl insults at Glenn, who had picked himself up off the pew and was brushing himself off, looking derisively at Sunday, who sobbed as she spoke, still struggling, and was basically hysterical.

Noah figured she could have gone to the doctor and gotten some tranquilizers or something to keep herself calm. But until Glenn had stood in front of her, she seemed to be doing just fine.

"Hey." He didn't know what else to say. He couldn't say "It's okay," because it wasn't. No one thought anything was okay. It was not okay when a child dies. He couldn't say, "you want to set a good example for your children," because her only child was lying cold in the casket.

He couldn't say, "calm down," because he didn't feel like he had that right. Maybe he could say that he would act the exact same way that she was, if he had been in her situation, but he didn't really see how that would help.

He pulled her aside as the crowd formed around them. He recognized Lena, her mother, as she hurried over, deep lines of concern etched in her brow as she held her hands out, effectively taking Sunday from his arms.

He didn't laugh, it would have been a humorless laugh, but he'd finally gotten to hold Sunday. Although he hadn't even really noticed. He was just trying to...keep her from killing her ex, he supposed.

He wanted to comfort her. To be the one who had that right, but he stepped back, giving room to her mother, who barely glanced at him.

He recognized several of her brothers who had arrived at her side, two of them down on one knee in front of her, their hands on her shoulder and leg as they spoke with her.

Noah continued to step back, giving room for the people who were closest to her. They would have the best idea of how to comfort and console her.

He'd come, done what he planned to do, and he supposed it was time for him to leave.

Turning, he started toward the back of the church. He walked down the center aisle which, once he got past the first several rows, was practically empty, as everyone had surged forward to see the excitement happening at the front.

His business partner, Franklin, stood at the back with his hands in his pockets, concern on his face.

Noah had left him out in the parking lot, but he obviously made his way in at some point.

"She okay?" Franklin asked as Noah reached his side.

"Probably not. I don't think I would be okay if I just lost my only child. I think that was her ex."

"Glenn?" Franklin asked. He'd grown up in Strawberry Sands as well, although Noah hadn't really become good friends with him until they'd been roommates in college.

They'd ended up spending the next four years almost inseparable, going to grad school together as well. It was only natural once they graduated that they started their own company together.

They might have been successful anyway, but Franklin's grandmother had died, leaving him a large inheritance.

Noah's family had sold property near Blueberry Beach, which had skyrocketed in value in the amount of time he was in college, and his parents had divided that up equally among their children.

It had been a nice little bump as they started business together. Although Noah figured that their business would not have been successful if they hadn't made good decisions, despite the fact that they started out with more money than most people did and did not have to lure investors or cater to their whims.

Noah looked back over his shoulder. He couldn't see Sunday; she was surrounded by family and friends. Glenn stood talking to the tall, slender woman whose face looked angry and not the slightest bit compassionate.

The little boy beside her jumped up and down, yanking on her arm, and there was something nasty about her face as she hissed at him to stop.

"Yeah. I'm pretty sure that was Glenn."

"He's aged well. Although, the lady he's with doesn't look too pleasant."

Noah jerked his head, and Franklin stepped back, giving him room to turn as they went shoulder to shoulder out of the church.

Franklin seemed to understand he was in a contemplative mood and didn't insist on conversation as they found Noah's car in the parking lot and got in.

They'd actually driven up from Chicago the previous day so they could meet with their team at the hotel site.

Noah had plans to move to Strawberry Sands, but he'd been in Chicago long enough that he hadn't heard about Sunday's loss until the day before. Franklin, who was riding with him, had thankfully agreed to take the time out to at least stop at, if not attend, the funeral.

"You and Sunday were pretty close in high school," Franklin finally commented, after they'd driven for a few minutes.

"I guess," he said. He didn't really want to talk about it. Although, Franklin's perspective was interesting, since they hadn't been great friends back then and he didn't know that Noah had had a huge crush on her. It wasn't something Noah went around telling people at this point in his life.

"I always thought you two would end up being a couple at some point, and then she got infatuated with Glenn."

Noah took a turn, looking at the horses in the field as they grazed, their tails swishing, their movements slow and languid. Relaxing. He was ready to come home. Ready to be back in Strawberry Sands. He looked out the windshield, where the lake, blue and beautiful, rolled in the distance.

If his child had drowned in that lake, would he want to continue to live beside it? Wouldn't he hate it?

Wouldn't it be the height of irony if he were moving back to Strawberry Sands only to have Sunday move away.

"Of course, Glenn was older, a good bit older, and I suppose he was romantic and dashing and all that stuff that women seem to like."

"Probably," Noah said, knowing that what Franklin said was true. He didn't have to like it though.

By the time they made it back to Chicago, their talk turned to business and plans, and Franklin never mentioned Sunday again. Noah's thoughts hardly left her. He wished there was something he could do. She was so grief stricken, so inconsolably bereaved, and he just wanted to help her. Maybe even if he hadn't had a crush on her, he would still be looking for something he could do to help.

As he walked into his condo in Chicago later that night, after dropping Franklin off, he still hadn't gotten the idea out of his mind that he wanted to do something to help.

He'd gone through his messages, answered some emails, and done a little bit of work on his laptop before grabbing some leftovers out of the fridge and taking a shower.

He sat in front of the big window that overlooked Lake Michigan, still with Sunday on his mind.

Restless, he got up, maybe out of habit opening cupboard doors and looking in them, like something had changed since the last time he'd seen them.

When he got to his junk drawer, he saw a notebook and pulled that out.

An idea started to form, and he looked for a pen.

He couldn't send her an email and couldn't send her a text, because he didn't have her email address or phone number, but Strawberry Sands was tiny. The little post office was only open for a few hours in the morning. Dorothy Miller had been the postmistress since he was a kid, and she had seemed old then. She knew everyone in Strawberry Sands, and if he got his letter to the post office with Sunday's name on it, Dorothy would make sure Sunday got it.

That was a great idea, but as he sat down, he wasn't sure what to say. What did he say to someone who lost their child? He wanted to make her feel better, but how did he do that?

Finally, after biting the end of the pencil for a while, he just started to write. Maybe, if it was terrible, he wouldn't send it. But his heart was just too full for him to not do anything.

Dear Sunday,

I was at the church today for the viewing. My heart hurt. I didn't know what to do or say. How do you tell someone that you're hurting for them? Especially someone you don't really know very well. But someone that your heart breaks for because you know they're going through a hard time.

You looked so calm and strong as you stood by the casket of your son, greeting people.

I knew you years ago, and I admired you then. I admired you today as well.

I suppose being a single mom is hard, and losing your only child must be devastating. I really don't know. I don't have children.

I felt terrible and wanted to do something. Something to make you feel better. But what could I do?

So I stayed for a bit, but even though you were greeting people, you seemed tired. I know if I had been standing as long as you had, my feet would hurt, and I'd want to sit down. Maybe it feels good to know that so many people love you and care about you, or maybe you wanted to be anywhere else. I don't know. But I didn't get in line.

Instead, I went and stood beside the casket for a few moments.

Your son was handsome.

Such a sweet boy. His hair was the same color as yours, and he had your chin.

Somehow it made me smile to see the toys that lined his casket. It seemed a little sad to send him away without anything, even though I know he's happy in heaven right now, playing with Jesus. I'm sure there are puppies in heaven. Puppies, horses, and, I don't know, maybe he and the other kids have chariot races or something. Do they drive cars in heaven?

Regardless, it makes my heart feel a little better to think of him there. But it gets heavy again when I think of him there and you here without him.

Anyway, I couldn't tell you everything that was in my heart, and I left without talking to you.

Still, you were on my mind the rest of the day, so I sat down this evening and decided I would write to you.

From where I sit, I can see Lake Michigan. I wonder if you hate it now. I suppose I probably would, even though I've loved it all of my life. I grew up beside it, swam in it when I was a kid, boated on it as a teenager, and spent more than one afternoon having business lunches with clients on it as an adult.

I guess I'll probably never look at it quite the same, but I'm not the kind of person who quits loving very easily. I suppose I'll always love the lake.

Anyway, I didn't say anything to you at the church, but this way I can say something to you while you're sitting down with your feet propped up, and you don't have to smile at me if you don't want to.

Just know I'm thinking about you and praying for you, and I admire you.

An acquaintance from long ago,

Business Boy

Noah looked at the letter and wished that there was some way he could see Sunday's reaction to it. He just wanted to make sure that he wasn't saying anything that would cause her pain or grief or heartache. He also wished that there was some way she could write him back if she wanted to.

But he couldn't put his name, couldn't put his return address on it. She might throw it in the trash can before she even read it. Of course, she might be happy to hear from an old friend too.

But for some reason, he just wanted to remain anonymous. Without the emotional entanglement of their high school friendship and the way it ended so abruptly, because of the man she'd been in a fight with earlier.

Finally, he decided there was nothing to do for it, except deliver it to the Strawberry Sands post office himself. He could rent a box at the post office and specifically ask Mrs. Miller to not tell anyone whose it was.

He thought he could trust her. He supposed she gossiped some, but never maliciously, and he felt like she would respect his request.

With that settled, he folded the paper, found an envelope, and wrote Sunday's name on it.

Franklin and he had been talking about moving to Strawberry Sands anyway. Him because he wanted out of the rat race, and Franklin... Maybe Franklin wanted out too. Although he had never said, not to Noah anyway. But they both wanted to see their hotel go up.

Making a note to himself to see what Franklin said in the morning, he set the letter on his counter and said another short prayer for Sunday, thinking of her after the funeral and how terrible she must be feeling, asking the Lord to comfort her and keep her close.

<h1 style="text-align:center">Chapter 3</h1>

Sunday pulled the pillow over her head. It had been a week since Blake's funeral, and she'd barely gotten out of bed.

She was staying in the attic room at her mother's bed-and-breakfast. She hadn't been back to her apartment since Blake had...

She tried not to think about it. She could see the lake, see him falling, hear as he yelled, and watch as he disappeared underneath the water, the wave crashing back over him, pulling him out even as another wave came in.

She swallowed, unable to cry anymore. Her eyes burned, her throat hurt, and she continuously felt like she was going to throw up. Just a sickness in her stomach that wouldn't go away.

She rolled over, tucking her head under the blankets, burying her face in her pillow, sobbing without tears.

She didn't care. Didn't care about life, didn't care about getting up, didn't care about anything. She had never understood people who wanted to die, but that's where she was.

Lord. Take me home. I want to be with Blake.

"Good morning!" Her mother's voice drifted through the blankets sometime later, although Sunday wasn't sure how long.

"I'm fine. Go away." The blankets muffled her voice, but she didn't care. She hadn't heard her mother climb the stairs to the attic, like she had every morning before. She brought Sunday food, encouraged her to eat and drink, trying to get her out of bed.

Sunday had drunk a little, but she hadn't eaten anything at all.

"Now, honey. It's been a week. I know you need time to grieve, but there's a reason God left you here, and you need to find it."

Her mother's voice still held compassion, but it also held an edge of encouragement or maybe just a warning that Sunday had reached the limits of what she could push. She remembered that tone as a child. Where her mother had maybe indulged her a little but was done.

"I'll get up tomorrow." She had said that yesterday and the day before.

"I have something for you. I want you to see it."

Her mother's voice was all business, and Sunday sighed inside. She wasn't going to get out of this. She could argue, but it would just be easier to do what her mother wanted and then get back under the covers and hide from the world. Try to get away from the pain. And the memories. And the idea that she should have done better. She should have made a different decision. She could have prevented it if she had just done things differently.

"Come on, Sunday. It's time for you to at least make a bit of an effort to pull yourself out of this funk."

"It's not a funk, Mom. I lost my kid." Sunday couldn't help the anger that leapt into her voice as her eyes narrowed at the mother she loved with her whole heart. Couldn't she understand? Didn't she know that her world revolved around Blake?

"I didn't mean to minimize what you're going through. Funk, depression, total devastation. I know you're hurting. I know that life is hard after a blow like this, but... You're not done with life. You'll see Blake again. And for now, you still have a job to do."

Her mother's words were soft and more compassionate than irritated.

Sunday knew her mom knew what she was talking about. After all, Lena had her husband walk out on her while she had five little kids to take care of. She hadn't had time to bury her head in her bed and spend a week crying.

Sunday understood that devastation. Her husband had done the same thing. It wasn't anything compared to losing a child.

But what if she had had other children? What if she had lost one child and still had another child to take care of?

Thankfully she didn't, but she knew there were people who had. People who had no choice but to go on.

It must be possible. It must be.

She felt tired and lethargic and weak as her stomach roiled, but she pushed the covers back, rolled, and struggled to a semi-sitting position.

Her mother sat down on the side of the bed. "I brought you some broth. I thought that would be easier on your stomach."

The words made Sunday want to cry again. Her mother was being such a good mother. The kind of mother she wanted to be. Except her son was gone.

She swallowed hard, but she couldn't keep the tears from dripping out of her eyes.

"Oh, honey. I wish I could do this for you. It just kills me to see you like this."

She hated that she was causing her own mother grief. Her sadness felt so big and so heavy and so black and so unbear-able, she didn't wish it on anyone. Didn't wish even a portion of it on anyone.

"I was out for a walk this morning, and I got some more espresso beans. I know that food is not supposed to be some-thing we lean on for comfort, but since coffee doesn't seem to be settling in your stomach very well, I thought maybe these would work."

Her mom set a little cup with ten or so beans in it on the nightstand beside her bed.

The kind gesture made Sunday's eyes fill up yet again.

"Please stop being nice to me. I can't stand it." Her voice cracked, and she swiped at her eyes again. They were sore from all the tears she already shed. Her skin was chapped, and it burned. She couldn't seem to stop.

"I'm sorry. I can't be anything but kind. I guess you need someone with a drill sergeant mentality."

"Yeah. Someone to just kick my butt and be mean to me so I don't keep thinking about how much I love my mother and how much I loved being a mother. How much I wanted to be a mother just like you." Her voice was watery, her eyes still dripping.

"I've been praying for you. But I know the best thing that you can do right now is to make yourself get up. You be the drill sergeant. Don't allow yourself to wallow. You have to get out of the wallowing and put yourself back in life. I know it's a cliché, but time really does make it not hurt quite so much."

She hoped so. She couldn't wait for a whole lot of time to pass so she wasn't hurting anymore. Until the pain could dull some. She didn't realize that a non-physical blow could hurt so much.

"I'll try," she finally said. More to get her mother out of the room than because she actually wanted to get herself out of bed. Even though she knew her mother was right. She needed to be a drill sergeant. She needed to force herself to ignore the pain and get on with life. She could come to grips with it eventually. A little bit at a time, rather than in big chunks.

"I'm afraid that if you keep wallowing, eventually the pit that you're in is going to be so deep you'll never be able to get out. You have to get out now while you still can." Her mother patted her arm and then brushed her hair away from her forehead the way she had when she was a little girl.

The way Sunday had brushed Blake's hair back so many times.

"I know you're right, Mom," Sunday said. She sighed inside. She didn't want to get better. She just wanted to lie there and be miserable.

"Oh. I thought this might cheer you up too," her mother said as she stood, digging in her apron pocket. "There was a letter at the post office for you. Dorothy Miller gave it to me. And I wanted to pass it on to you. I'll set it over here so you can't read it until you get up."

"Okay," Sunday said, although her voice lacked any excitement or enthusiasm or interest. It was probably just another well-wisher sending a card with some kind of pre-written verse on it that when she wasn't grieving, she would enjoy.

"I need you to help me clean today. We were full last night, and I actually turned some people away. It's coming on the busy season, and with Griff and Chi and their new Percheron team, interest in Strawberry Sands has doubled from last year." Her mother paused. "I could really use this room."

Her mother had never rented the room out before, and Sunday wondered if maybe that was a ploy to try to get her up. But she didn't want to keep her mom from making money. She worked so hard all her life, she deserved to be successful.

"All right. Maybe not today?"

Her mother smiled gently. "Not today. But if you can clean the green room and the blue room for me, that would be great."

"By noon?" Sunday asked, having no idea what time it was.

"Noon was an hour ago. Guests will be checking in by four o'clock. So sometime in the next three hours. Please."

That stunk. She was going to have to get out of bed, and not just sit in a chair in misery, but actually work. And in three hours, she had to clean two rooms. It took an hour for each room, so... She needed to get moving. Probably exactly what her mother intended.

"Okay. I... I'll do it." Sunday didn't want to say that, but she couldn't turn her mom down. Plus, she knew her mom was only trying to do what was best for her. But her mom couldn't help her get better.

Sunday was the only one who could make the decision to do the things she needed to do in order to pull herself out of the...funk, as her mom said. Funk was probably a better word than depression, though. She didn't want to admit that she was most likely depressed.

Her mom slipped out of her room, closing the door behind her, and Sunday was very tempted to roll over and pull the covers back over her head.

Her childhood training would not allow her to do that. She told her mom she would clean those rooms, and she couldn't let her mom down.

She should probably get a shower first, since she couldn't remember the last time she'd taken one, but the rooms were the most urgent thing on her schedule.

When she got those done, she could shower and crawl back in bed. It was only that promise—the promise of getting back in bed—that got her up. As she stood, she saw the little cup of espresso beans that her mom had set on her nightstand.

Her mom had gotten addicted to the things, and from what Sunday understood, they came from the man who owned the lighthouse on the beach. Well, not that man. He had a son who lived in Chicago, and apparently that son brought the man espresso beans, and he gave them to her mom.

It was quite the supply chain her mom had to feed her addiction, and it almost made Sunday smile.

Except she couldn't. She could never smile again. She would never be happy again. She would always be longing for heaven and to be reunited with her baby.

She couldn't believe after seven years he was gone. It felt like a wasted seven years. What was the point in midnight feedings, early-morning diaper changes, sleepless nights while she paced the floor praying his fever would go down, his cough would subside, his little body would fight whatever infection he had. Trips to the doctor, playdates, hours on her knees in prayer that she hadn't messed her son up for life when her husband had left her, and she had to raise him as a single mom.

Wondering if her poor choice of a husband was going to screw up her son for life. All of those things now seemed so pointless. It didn't matter. Nothing mattered.

Except... Her mom was right. She wasn't put on this earth to please herself. She wasn't even put on this earth to raise her son. She was put on this earth to bring glory to God. To serve him. To do His will. To choose Him above everything, even above her child.

Is that why You took him, Lord? Did I love him more than I loved You?

That seemed so...wrong. But who was she to say what was right and wrong? She didn't make the universe, she couldn't create a world. She didn't speak anything into existence. God did all of that. Was it not His right and prerogative to decide what was right and wrong?

She supposed it was also His prerogative to give and to take away as well.

It was just so hard to believe that He was a loving father when He allowed things like this to happen.

But she had to remind herself that He had created a perfect world to begin with. Things like this weren't supposed to happen. It was man's decision to sin. To believe the serpent, to eat the apple. Man was the one who caused the fall and allowed sin to enter into the perfect world. So then, bad things happened.

Except God, in His loving goodness, used those bad things to shape them and to grow them into people who were more like Jesus. Only if she allowed it.

She bit the insides of her cheeks and wrapped her arms around her waist. She didn't want to listen to reason. She didn't want to be reminded that God was good, and that everything would work out for her good and God's glory. She didn't want to think that there could be glory in her child's death.

Even though she knew it to be true.

Maybe, God just wanted to know if she would lift up her fingers and give Him everything. She liked to think she was a Christian. She liked to think she loved God and did what He told her to do. But if God asked her for something and she wasn't willing to give it to Him, didn't that mean that she wasn't really submitting to God's will? That she wasn't really giving up her own way and willing to live God's way?

She hadn't made her bed, hadn't even got her clothes changed. It had been an effort just to get up. But now, she dropped to her knees beside the bed and put her head on the mattress that was still warm from her body.

Lord.

She didn't know what to say. She had so much pain and grief and agony in her heart, she didn't know how to phrase an apology. Confession. A request for forgiveness for her stubbornness and for her desire to have what she wanted and to refuse to allow God to have His way.

She thought of the verse in the Bible. The one about God wanting a pierced heart and not sacrifice. He said to obey was better than sacrifice, and that took a humble, pierced heart.

Her heart felt pierced all right. But God wanted it to be for Him. He wanted her to humble herself under His authority and acknowledge that He was God and she would do what He wanted.

Even if that meant He took her child. She had to be okay with it.

Lord, my heart still hurts. I know You see that. Probably I'm going to cry a lot more too. I can't promise I won't. I don't think You expect me not to. But... But I know You have a plan. I know I haven't had a whole lot of faith in Your plan. I've been...angry... Because things didn't go the way I wanted them to. I'm still sad. I still long for my little boy. But I love You, and I know he's with You. And I know that You want the best for me. Please help me to live that and not just think that.

She stayed on her knees for a bit more. She didn't want her life to be just about her, where all her prayers were about her all the time, but maybe it was okay today if she didn't pray for anyone else except herself.

Except she knew she'd feel better if she tried to get her mind off herself and onto someone else. If she looked around to see who she could help, instead of curling in on herself and thinking about her own pain and grief.

Lord, be with Mom. Help me to be kind to her and bless her for being so good to people.

She thought about the hotel that was going in just north of town. How her mom had never said, but she was concerned about how it would take business away from her bed-and-breakfast. She wanted Strawberry Sands to grow just like everyone else, had wanted her son to grow up in a town that was thriving, but she didn't want to see her mom lose business either.

She prayed a bit more, trying to put a focus on others, and while she didn't want to dismiss the pain in her heart—she was allowed to feel pain—she didn't want to dwell on it either. Life was about more than just her.

Pushing to her feet, she realized she actually felt a little better. Maybe not...happy exactly, but better. She grabbed her covers, flipped them over her bed, and smiled when she noticed the cup of espresso beans. Her mom couldn't understand why the rest of the world didn't think these things were the most awesome things in the entire universe, the way she did. It made Sunday smile, as cute as her mom was.

She reached into the cup and pulled out an espresso bean, even though she didn't really care for them. It would make her mom happy to know that she at least tried to eat. And knowing her mom, she'd counted the beans before she put them in the cup.

Sunday ate a couple; it would make her mom smile.

She munched on the beans as she finished smoothing out the blankets on the bed.

She turned to her dresser, thinking she wanted to get clothes out that she could work in, since she had two rooms to clean, and maybe she could help her mom with some other things.

Although she felt a lot better than she had just half an hour ago, she figured that there were still going to be lows along with highs. Still, if she could get her thinking aligned in the right direction, hopefully her actions would follow.

She opened the top drawer of the dresser to pull out some clean clothes when her eyes landed on the letter her mother had brought in. It wasn't a card like she had expected. But an actual letter. Her address was handwritten on the front, and the return address... She squinted and tilted her head to try to read it. There was no name. Just a PO Box number. For Strawberry Sands. Odd. She didn't recognize the handwriting, although that wasn't shocking. People didn't send letters anymore, and she didn't see too many people's handwriting anymore.

Everyone typed or texted.

Grabbing her shirt and some underthings, she shut the drawer, picked out a pair of pants from another drawer, and grabbed the letter, looking at it as she walked over to her bed.

She thought maybe she would wait to read it until after she cleaned the rooms. It would give her something to look forward to. But maybe she could think about the letter and write a response later.

And then she realized it was the first thing she'd actually been interested in in a week. So, setting her clothes on her bed, she sat down slowly and opened the letter, wondering the entire time who it could possibly be from.

It was handwritten. She could hardly believe it. And then she began to read.

When she was finished, there were tears rolling down her cheeks, but they were good tears, she thought. Tears that someone she barely even knew had been prompted to write a letter, to ease her grief, to make her feel better. That was kind of him.

Setting the letter aside, she finished dressing and grabbed two more espresso beans on her way out the door. She managed to get both rooms cleaned by three fifteen, meeting her mom once in the hall.

Her mom smiled at her, and Sunday thought there might actually have been tears in her eyes as well.

She hated that her mom had been so worried. But she couldn't change it now.

All she could do was to try to lean on the Lord and have faith in His plan, putting one foot in front of the other, knowing that she needed to go on with her life.

She showered when she got back to her room, seeing the letter still lying on her nightstand where she left it. It hadn't been far from her thoughts. And she wanted to answer. To send a reply. To thank the person for taking the time to not just give her a few words of comfort after everybody else had left her but actually write a letter and send it to her a week later, when she really needed it.

It actually took her mind off Blake and all the pain and grief.

With a towel around her hair and another one around her body, she grabbed the notebook out of the bottom of her nightstand, along with the pen, and sat down in the little chair by the window. She tapped the pen against the windowsill and looked at the lake as she thought about what to write.

> Dear Business Boy,
>
> I don't hate the lake.
>
> Like you, I've always loved it. It's funny, because I didn't even think about blaming the lake. I blamed myself.
>
> I realized today, though, that blaming myself took a lot of credit for myself and didn't give God any. I guess I knew God could have saved my son, and maybe I was a little bit angry about that.

Okay. A lot angry.

But God is God. He created me. He created Blake. He has every right to take Blake whenever He wants to. Who am I to think that just because I love Blake, that means that God shouldn't have the right to take him from me? I didn't give Blake breath. I didn't form him while he was growing inside of me. It didn't take any thought on my part to create that baby at all. God did it. He did everything. Who am I to think that He should have done it differently? Or that He should do anything differently?

I realized how arrogant I was being. That I wanted to dictate to God how life should go. I have no right to do that. I have no right to do anything other than submit to His will and accept what He gives me.

Of course, I can pray for a different outcome. I can pray for changes. For example, my mom owns a bed-and-breakfast. Maybe you know it. She is concerned that the new hotel going up outside of Strawberry Sands will take business away from her.

I worry about that some too. But isn't that arrogant again? Shouldn't I be acting like whatever God allows to happen will be a good thing? Don't I trust Him?

I know it's taken a long time for whoever's putting the hotel in to get all the approvals that they need. There were times where I prayed that it would be denied. But they weren't. God knows.

He puts the people in power, and He takes them away too. It's just my job to pray that those people make wise decisions. I have to admit, I didn't pray that they would make wise decisions. I prayed that they would make the decisions that I wanted them to make. The Bible says that the powers that be are ordained by God.

Again, my thinking just wasn't quite aligned with the way God wants me to behave.

Anyway, your letter made me think, and I wanted to let you know that I still look at the lake and think it's beautiful. I look at the lake, and I'm amazed at God's power and majesty. I look at the lake, and I can't believe that God just spoke it into existence. It's amazing to me.

I'm also coming around to the idea that I don't need to hold on to the guilt that I feel. It wasn't that I was a bad mom. Even though it feels that way. It was that God allowed it to happen. I was being diligent, I was watching my son. I just took my eyes off him for a few seconds to look at the horses, and there's nothing wrong with that. I could have been watching him, and I still wouldn't have been able to save him. Not if it was the Lord's will for him to go.

Anyway, this letter ended up being a lot longer than what I expected. The only other thing I wanted to say was thank you for writing. I appreciate your concern for me at the funeral. It was a hard day. I'm not gonna lie.

But I think the harder days were after that. When everyone left and I felt alone. That's when I missed Blake the most.

Your letter came at a perfect time. Thank you for writing it.

Sincerely,

Lover of the lake

Chapter 5

Noah held the letter in his hand. She'd written back. She'd written back, and she seemed like she was better. At least, that she'd worked through the things she needed to work through, and that she was coming out on the other side.

She did not invite him to write again. But she had said that she had felt alone, after everyone left and the funeral was over.

Maybe she wouldn't mind another letter.

He continued down the street, tucking the letter in his pocket and pulling out his phone to answer several texts that had come in while he was reading.

By the time he was done with that, he had made it to the end of the sidewalk, and he stood looking over the lake, at the horses in the pasture on either side, and further up the hill to his right, he could see a set of dapple-gray Percheron mares grazing majestically.

He had been overjoyed when he found out that Griff and Chi had decided to not just move the diner to a better location but also invest in the Percherons. What a great addition to Strawberry Sands.

He stood taking the scene in, appreciating the beauty, glad he had decided to come back.

Glancing again at his phone, he saw that it was time to meet Franklin at the diner. He hurried across the street and opened the door, figuring he would grab a seat for Franklin and himself and peruse the new menu. He'd been in once or twice since they moved it, but Griff had unveiled an entire new menu at the beginning of the month, and Noah hadn't been in to try anything yet.

His heart almost stopped beating when he saw Sunday sitting at a booth, deep in conversation with Kristin, the woman who owned the biggest house in town. He thought she had maybe turned it into an assisted care center, since there seemed to be a good many older ladies that hung out around the place.

Noah figured he probably spent a little bit too much time in Strawberry Sands if he knew the business of everyone up and down the street.

But he didn't spend too much time dwelling on that, because his eyes were drawn to Sunday. It had been two weeks since the funeral. Almost three weeks since she lost her son.

Even from this distance, he could tell she had lost weight. Her eyes were sallow, and her face pinched, but there was a bit of a smile around her mouth as she spoke with Kristin.

Kristin reached across the table and put her hand over top of Sunday's, and that made both corners of Sunday's lips turn up.

Noah's heart turned over. He was glad she was doing so well.

He faced their table and could see her. She hadn't looked up when he walked in, and she didn't look at him now.

Part of him was glad about that, because he could watch her as much as he wanted to, part of him wanted her to notice him.

The conversation must have taken a turn, because Sunday's eyes filled with tears.

"Hey there. You're early. I guess that's normal. Which is why I try to be early, but somehow you always beat me." Franklin slid into the seat opposite Noah at the booth, effectively blocking his view of Sunday.

"Hey, man," he said, wishing he could move to the right or to the left to keep Sunday in his view.

Then he shook the thought away. He was here to talk business with his friend, and he needed to make sure he was giving his all for what he was doing. He couldn't allow himself to be sidetracked by a woman. Even if she was one that held a special place in his heart and always would.

"I heard they're getting some type of buggy that the horses can pull, that will go on sand."

"A buggy on sand?" Noah's attention was pulled back to his friend.

"That's what I heard. Something about the tires."

"Hello, fellows," Chi said as she walked to the table. "Good to see you guys today."

"Good to be back in Strawberry Sands," Noah said, meaning every word.

"How's the moving coming?" she asked as she pulled her notepad out of her apron pocket.

"I'm looking for a place. Do you know of one?"

Chi laughed a little. "If you want a small, one-bedroom apartment, there are two of them for rent over top of the old diner. That's where I lived before Griff and I got married. And if you don't want them, you can spread the word around."

"I'll take it." Noah didn't need to think about it. He'd move into the apartment while he looked for property. He already knew there weren't any houses for sale close enough. And he was kind of thinking he'd like to build a house on the beach. Nothing fancy, just something with a great view.

"Did you say there were two of them?" Franklin asked.

"I did. One has three rooms. Potentially it could be a two-bedroom apartment.

The other one is a one-bedroom. They're both small."

"I'll take the two-bedroom, unless Noah wanted it. My brother Peter talked about moving to town. He bought a farm just outside of Strawberry Sands, but it doesn't have a house on it."

"I see. Well, I was not thinking I was gonna rent out both apartments in one fell swoop and today of all days," Chi said with a laugh.

"Looks like that's what you did. You have to let us know the details."

"I can do that. But I can take your orders and get your food started first."

They gave their drink orders, and she walked away, promising to be back to chat about the apartments. Noah wasn't worried about it. She wouldn't be asking much for it, and he could afford to pay whatever she wanted. It would just be that he would be that much closer to Sunday, and he wasn't expecting that. But he couldn't say he was upset about it.

"I don't know. There are a lot of people working from home now, but do we really want to move two hours away from the city?" Franklin said after she left.

Franklin was a little more tied to the business or maybe just a little more into the city life than Noah was. Funny that he would have a brother who was all about farming.

"If you're getting cold feet, you don't have to. But I'm ready to get out. Every time I come back here, it just feels more and more like home. I didn't really want to leave to begin with. But there weren't any opportunities for people to make a living here when I was a kid. Now, with the ability to work from home as long as we have internet, the door is open, and I'm going to walk through."

"I'll miss the restaurants. I like good food."

"This new menu looks pretty good to me. And Griff is amazing in the kitchen."

"It's all his strawberry recipes that I really like."

"I don't know, that onion soup bread smells amazing. That's the special today, and I think I could probably just order a whole loaf and consider that my meal."

"Think of the carbs, man."

Noah snorted. Growing up, he didn't even know what a carb was.

He remembered what Sunday's letter had said, including one of the things that he wanted to bring up with Franklin.

"When we talked about the hotel, we said we wanted to benefit the people of Strawberry Sands, not just make money for us. I just heard today that the owner of the bed-and-breakfast is a little concerned that we'll take away her customers."

"People who stay at a bed-and-break-fast are different customers than people who stay at hotels."

"I know. But I'd like to ease her worry if we can."

"You have an idea?"

"Well, I just found out today, but I was thinking the hotel can put brochures for the bed-and-breakfast in the lobby. We can have directions, pricing, contact info, and even write up a history of the bed-and-breakfast. Lena had her hus-band walk out on her, and she was able to keep the farm together and still run the bed-and-breakfast. That's a great story."

"I remember that vaguely. That is quite a story. And people love stories. I think we could work it."

"Me too. I can see if she offers anything else. I don't know if she makes soaps or candles or sells canned goods or something. But we could even carry some of her wares in the lobby. Actually, anyone in Strawberry Sands who has a business could have it advertised in our lobby."

"That's a great idea!" Franklin was more about the business aspect, but he loved Strawberry Sands too. They had both agreed that they wanted their investment to benefit the community and not be a hindrance. Noah smiled at his excitement.

"All right. We'll keep thinking about other things we can do. But in the meantime, maybe one of us can go and talk to Lena."

"I've got a meeting at three in Chicago. So if you want to do it today, it's going to have to be you."

"All right. I'll do it." It wouldn't be a hardship to go to Lena's. He knew Sunday had her own place above the candy shop, but as far as he knew, the candy shop was still closed and Sunday had been staying with her mom.

They continued to talk, with Franklin pulling out his briefcase and spreading papers over their table. When Chi came back with their drinks, they stopped to discuss the specifics of renting their apartments. She understood that it was only going to be until they could find or build houses of their own.

Noah didn't want to mislead her. He'd already started looking at land, and there were several places where he would like to make an offer once they had things with the hotel running smoothly.

The entire time he was in the restaurant though, he was aware of Sunday and that she was just a little ways away.

Therefore, when he and Franklin walked out together, shaking hands before Franklin walked to his car, Noah walked on down to the beach.

He found a place to sit on the dunes, where he could see the horses and the water both, and then he pulled out his notebook and pen. Before he left for Chicago, he was going to drop a letter in the mail.

Dear Lover of the lake,

I like that you signed your letter that way, because I think you really meant what you said. You don't hate the lake. I suppose as much as that, I was worried that you might have bad memories associated with it. But that doesn't seem to be the case either. I haven't lost a lot of people in my life, so I'm not sure, but I know I can tell you where I was when I heard bad news. It seems to be forever associated with the place that you were when you heard it. I cannot imagine having it happen to you. Those associations would probably be strong.

Regardless, we definitely have that in common.

I wasn't sure whether it was okay for me to write you back or not. I don't want to bother you if you're busy. Or if you prefer not. But I guess it's partly from my desire to help. You said my letter came at a good time, and back when people used to send actual mail, it was always fun to get something in the mailbox other than bills. So I thought maybe if I continue to write, you would continue to smile when you saw that you got a letter.

Anyway, let me know if that's okay.

Also, I think the people who are building the hotel want to be careful that they don't take business away from Strawberry Sands. They're building it to help the community, not hurt it. From what I understand, they're going to have brochures in the lobby with your mother's bed-and-breakfast on it. I think someone is going to con-tact her so she can help design the brochures.

Noah looked out across the lake. Up the beach, three people rode horses right along the sand where the waves crashed on the shore. The view was majestic and pretty.

Did he want to tell Sunday who he was?

Part of him thought that maybe there were deeper feelings of antagonism toward the people who were bringing the hotel in. She was concerned about her mother's business; she might not have good feelings about someone who was potentially going to take it away.

He decided not to.

But that didn't mean that he couldn't put a plug in for the "businessmen who were building it." He smiled. He didn't want to manipulate Sunday or deceive her, but the purpose of the letters was to make her feel better.

Someone might be in contact with you. I... I'm not sure if you still have your candy shop open, but if you're interested in promoting it, I'm pretty sure the owners of the hotel are interested in having anyone with a busi-

ness in Strawberry Sands in their lobby.

I'm not going to be too long, because I don't know whether you want me to keep writing or not. If I don't hear from you again, I'll assume that it's a no. Thanks again for your letter. It made me smile. I'm glad you're doing better.

Sincerely,
Business Boy

Chapter 6

Sunday walked into her mom's bed-and-breakfast. She just had lunch with Kristin at the diner, and it had been bittersweet. Some laughter, some tears, and a sweet hour with a beautiful friend who truly cared about her.

It had done her so much good.

Not so much good that she felt like she could go to the candy shop or step into her apartment. Not just yet.

So she was back at her mom's house.

Her mom usually took a walk in the morning to go see her lighthouse friend, to check on him and make sure he was okay. At least that's what she said. Sunday figured that she took a walk just so she could be sure she got stocked up on her espresso bean habit.

But whatever it was, she had promised her mom that she would be at the bed-and-breakfast to answer the phone and take care of any request the guests who were staying over might have.

Her mom had left ten minutes ago, and so she didn't expect her back for two hours.

She busied herself in the kitchen, taking the canisters and Tupperware out of the cabinets and wiping them down.

She couldn't just sit and do nothing. She had to stay busy. Right now, anyway. If she didn't stay busy, she would end up thinking about Blake. And since she had gotten out of bed a week ago, she had been doing a lot better.

"Excuse me. Is Miss Lena around?"

She startled, turning so quickly she stumbled off the step stool she stood on and tripped. The canister of flour she held slipped from her fingers as she caught herself on the counter. It fell to the floor in a cloud of dust.

"Oh!" she said, barely keeping herself upright, as her eyes landed on the mess on the floor. Just what she needed to do in front of a potential customer. She was supposed to welcome them, not chase them away with flour canisters and messes.

"I'm sorry. I didn't mean to scare you," the man said, and his voice was rich and smooth and soothing.

Her hand rested over her heart as she slowly straightened from the counter and looked him over.

He had on business attire, casual. No tie, and the top button of his shirt was unbuttoned. He wore dress pants, but instead of the typical business shoes, he had on a pair of cowboy boots.

Her eyes caught on those, and they made her smile. She tried to hide it as her eyes came back up to his face.

He looked a little familiar.

"Do I know you?" she blurted out. She could blame it on Blake. Or the stress of the last few weeks. She didn't typically greet guests like that.

"Actually, you do. I'm Noah. Noah Sterner." He opened his mouth to say more, but she gasped.

"Noah? From high school?"

He nodded.

"Goodness. It's been years." She couldn't keep the pleasure out of her voice. Her memories of her time with Noah were all sweet. He had been a good friend. She crinkled her brow. "I can't even remember the last time I talked to you. I guess we just drifted apart." After graduation? She couldn't really remember.

And then it hit her.

Glenn.

"I always felt bad for the way I just kind of left everyone when I fell head over heels for Glenn." She took a breath. This wasn't something she was expecting to have to say today. "I owe you an apology."

Here he was, at the bed-and-breakfast, and she wasn't letting him state his business, she was dredging up old memories. But now that she'd started, she had to finish. "Sorry. I valued your friendship, but I didn't act like I did."

He grunted a little laugh. "Don't worry about it. I certainly don't hold anything against you. I... Sorry things didn't work out."

He seemed truly unhappy. And that was Noah. He'd always been concerned about others. As she recalled, his family had money, but he never acted like it. He'd always been humble. And that appealed to her. It made her feel better that he wasn't holding her past against her.

"It's okay. That's water under the bridge. And nothing I can do about it now. But I do feel bad that I pretty much dumped the people who cared about me and ran off with someone who didn't in the end."

"I think we've all made stupid mistakes like that."

"You've been married?" He certainly seemed like the kind of man who would have a wife and a couple of kids in a happy home. Somewhere. Noah was loyal. She remembered that much.

"No. Never been."

She let that sink in. She wasn't sure exactly what that meant. But his eyes held hers, and she couldn't think of anything else to say.

Finally, he cleared his throat and said, "So, I was here to talk to your mom. She still owns the bed-and-breakfast, right?"

"Yeah. She does. But I'm here right now, because she's taking a walk." She took a breath. Why did she feel so odd? Light-headed? Maybe she needed to eat more. "Can I help you with something?"

"I wanted to ask her about making a brochure, but let me help you get this flour cleaned up first. Someone else might come in, and I'm sure you'd feel better if the kitchen looked less dusty."

She laughed. She'd totally forgotten about the flour on the floor. That showed how jumbled her brain was.

"All right." She pointed to the pantry where they kept the broom and dust-pan. "Do you mind grabbing the broom and dustpan from there, and I'll scoop up as much of this as I can and get it in the trash."

He jerked his head, set his briefcase down well away from the flour mess, and walked to the pantry.

By the time he came back with the broom and dustpan, she'd gotten several large handfuls of flour off the floor and tossed them in the trash.

He swept up everything that was left on the floor while she grabbed the rag to wipe down the counters and the covered doors and swipe at what was left on the floor.

Five minutes later, the kitchen looked the way it had before she showered it with flour.

"Thanks for your help. Honestly, we don't usually put guests to work around here."

"I like to think I'm a little more than a guest. I used to be a friend."

There was something in his tone that made her eyes sweep to his.

"You're still a friend. A friend with a lot of years between us, but still a friend."

She smiled. She liked that he hadn't hesitated to help. That's what friends did, right? They jumped in when they were needed. They didn't sit around and wait for her to finish up and then hurry out to help them. But dug in and worked beside her.

Maybe Noah was just a natural friend to everyone.

The thought didn't exactly make her happy, even though she knew it should. She liked that he had made her feel special. She wanted to continue to feel special to him. That she was a little different. Maybe because they had history; they had shared memories, and they were good ones.

"All right. Thanks so much." She dusted her hands off on her apron and then nodded in the direction of the dining room. "We can talk in there if it's okay. Guests might come through, but I need to be here to talk to them anyway in case they need anything."

"That's good. Lead the way."

Chapter 7

Noah followed Sunday into the dining room. He hadn't expected to find her in the kitchen at the bed-and-breakfast. Maybe he'd hoped he might catch a glimpse of her, but he hadn't expected that he'd be sitting and talking to her.

It had been gratifying to see that she remembered him. That she looked pleased to see him. Like the memories were good. He was afraid the reference to Glenn might throw her off, but it hadn't, and she'd apologized. He hadn't been expecting that. It showed a humbleness he admired.

"It's okay to sit here?" she asked as she indicated the head of the dining room table while she pulled out a chair for herself beside it.

"This is perfect." He sat down, pulled the little bit that he'd printed out on a piece of paper out of his briefcase, and set it down in front of him. "I'm not sure if you know that it's me and my partner who are building the hotel just north of Strawberry Sands."

"No!" Her eyes were wide, her hand went to her chest. It didn't look like she was very happy about it.

He hurried to explain. "My friend and I are doing it because we both grew up in Strawberry Sands... You probably remember Franklin Slessing."

She nodded, but she hadn't relaxed.

"We love it here. I'm moving back. Love the small town, love the lake views, love the camaraderie that you find here. I even love the winters."

She laughed a little, because there were a lot of people who did not love the winters.

"But it's hard for anyone who grows up here to stay here and make a living."

"I can't disagree with that. I've been trying for three years to get my candy shop to take off, and if it hadn't been for my mom hiring me to help her here at the bed-and-breakfast, I wouldn't have been able to stay here."

"Exactly. We're hoping that the hotel will draw tourists, particularly in the summer. The Percheron team that Chi and Griff have purchased have been a huge draw along with the horseback riding. I understand they have someone close to them managing it."

"Rodney. He's...just graduated from high school. He might be going to college, but yeah. He loves the horses."

He nodded. He heard stories, but they were rumors. So he didn't want to mention it. But it seemed like Rodney maybe had a tough time, and the horses were good for him. Regardless, it didn't really apply to the subject at hand. He was talking about the hotel.

"We want to help the people of Strawberry Sands. I mean, I'm not gonna sit here and tell you that we're going to do it at a loss. We're not. We want to make money. But drawing people in, giving them a place to stay should help with the tourism aspect. But we don't want to take business away from your mother."

"That's a relief," she said, but her words were guarded.

"One of the things that we were thinking that would help would be to have a brochure in the lobby with all of the information about the bed-and-breakfast. Your mom has a great story, a story of overcoming. It's a story of achieving the

American dream, pretty much. Without the romance aspect, I guess."

Sunday snorted. "A lot of us don't have the romance aspect."

She sounded a little bitter, but Noah didn't comment on that. He wanted to. Wanted to ask her if the right man came along, if she would consider trying the romance thing again.

He wanted to try for the first time. But only with her.

He shook those thoughts away. He was supposed to be focusing on the brochure and the hotel.

"Anyway. We wanted to give it a promi-nent place in the hotel. Personally, in my experience and to my business knowledge, the people who stay in hotels are different than the people who stay at bed-and-breakfasts. The hotel shouldn't be taking business away. But my partner and I agreed that we won't be offering free breakfast at the hotel. If people want breakfast, they'll have to stay with you."

"I like that," she said cautiously.

"We'll also have the brochure, and that was what I wanted you to help me design. Or Lena. One of you."

"Well, Mom's in charge, but she often delegates to us kids. I'm pretty sure that one of us will be doing it, most likely me."

He laughed and was gratified to see her smiling. She had a beautiful smile. Not necessarily because she had perfect features, but more because it lit up her face, made her eyes glow, and warmed his heart. That was what made her smile so amazing.

"All right then. I just told you my ideas, you're welcome to come up with something else. I can have my people design it with your ideas, or you guys can design it yourselves. It's totally up to you."

"All right." Her eyes went to the paper in front of him where he'd typed out the information he thought should be on it. "I assume we have some time to think about this? Considering the hotel isn't even built?"

"I'm hoping to have it done by the end of the summer. It should go up fast, now that we've cleared all the hurdles with the state and local authorities. We have everything lined up, and construction began last week."

"Wow. I thought it would take years to build. Shows what I know."

"It takes years to get permission to build." He loved the glow in her eyes. And he loved that she wasn't afraid to admit when she didn't know something. Again, it showed a humbleness that he didn't always see in people. But he appreciated.

"You know, I never saw you as a businessman. I guess I thought you'd stay around Strawberry Sands. Although, you have a point. I don't know what you would have done to earn a living."

"Me either. My parents ended up with some property that brought in a lot of money. My grandparents weren't exactly rich, but they were well off. My dad was able to work from home, back before it was something that everybody did. So, I guess that's how I was able to grow up here. But there wasn't anything for me to take over or step into, so I had to make my own way."

"So many of us do. But I guess I was blessed." She looked around the room. "I had this to fall back on. Thankfully. Since my candy shop isn't doing very well."

"We'll put a brochure for your candy shop in the hotel too. We want to do all the businesses that are in Strawberry Sands. Like I said, we're promoting the town, not just the hotel, because what benefits Strawberry Sands benefits us."

"That makes sense to me. I guess... I haven't been back in my candy shop because I live above it and..."

"I heard about your loss. I'm sorry."

He hated to bring it up, although she really had. Because she'd gone from smiling with her eyes sparkling to looking down at her hands on the table and seeming sad.

"Thank you. I'm not over it, not by any stretch. But every day, I feel a little better, you know? Mom said time heals everything; I didn't believe that could be true. It's funny, when you hear that, you want a whole lot of time to pass really fast. But that's not the point, is it?"

"I think maybe sometimes we have to go through grief so that we can help other people who are going through grief."

"I know God has a reason. Maybe that's it."

"I hope not. It's hard to watch others suffer. I know for myself, I'd rather go through it for them than watch people I love be miserable."

"That's what my mom says. I suppose I feel the same way. Or...felt. With my son. I couldn't stand it when he was hurting. I wanted to hurt instead. Take it on me, you know?"

Boy, did he ever. He had wanted to take her hurt since he first heard about it, and they weren't even that close. It was just a long-standing infatuation, crush... Those words didn't seem to be the right words. Regardless, it was a long-standing admiration that he had for her, and he didn't want to see her hurt. Not at all.

"Yeah. But life doesn't work that way."

"That was something else I had to learn. I mean, I already knew it, that God is in charge and life doesn't work the way we want it to or think it should. I mean, if I were as wise as God, I could create a world and make the rules for it. But I can't. And so I have to admit that and submit to God's rules."

"That sounds hard, until we remember that the Bible tells us over and over again that God is love. He is love."

"Exactly. And not only is He loving, He's kind, long-suffering, and He wants the best for us. He's gone out of His way, over and over again, to make sure that He could have a relationship with us. And He's shown, over and over again, that everything He does is for our good."

"And His glory. I think we forget that a lot. We think that life is about making ourselves happy. But it's supposed to be about giving God glory."

"And somehow that makes us happy. Isn't it crazy the way that works?"

"And that's how you know the Bible is true. Because when you actually put those principles to work, things that don't make any sense, like us not living for ourselves, giving God glory, and other things like forgiving and being kind...

They end up being better for us than what we realized."

"Not just good for us mentally, but scientists are finding out that it's good for us physically as well. And God knew it all along."

Noah nodded. "Don't you think sometimes it's sad the way we have such a hard time trusting God, even though He's proven Himself over and over again to be trustworthy? If I were God, I wouldn't have patience for that. I'd be like, 'Don't you get it already?'"

She laughed, as he intended, and he felt better that they were back on solid ground. She was no longer sad. Although, after going through what she had, it was totally understandable that she would have times where she wasn't happy. It was completely allowed.

They spent a little bit more time talking about brochures, with Sunday promising that she would work on them and talk to her mother about them.

He gave her his number. And he also refrained from telling her that he'd been wanting to give her his number for years. Decades.

She punched it into her phone, and shortly after that, his phone buzzed.

"Excuse me."

"That's probably just me. I sent you a text so you have my number too."

His hand stilled on his phone, without picking it up.

And he had hers.

It was like a dream come true. He shouldn't put too much stock in it. Obviously, he shouldn't. It was a business transaction, but... Maybe things actually were going to go in the direction that he wanted them to for so long.

He thought about asking her out for dinner. Could he do it?

"Have you seen the new menu at the diner?" he asked as he gathered his paper and put it back in his briefcase.

"I was just there today."

"I saw you." Maybe he shouldn't have said that. Because she obviously hadn't seen him.

Her eyes got big. "Really? You were there?"

"I was sitting a couple of booths down. You were talking to a friend, someone I recognized. Kristin?"

"Yes. Kristin."

"You guys were in deep discussion. I thought I was going to be talking to your mom. If I had realized that I needed to talk to you, I could have saved myself the hassle of walking the couple of blocks up the sidewalk."

"That wasn't a big hassle."

"No. It wasn't. And I enjoyed my time with you."

"It was nice to see you again."

This was his opportunity. He took a breath. And clenched the handle of his briefcase.

"Would you like to have dinner at the diner sometime?"

Her eyes got big, and he realized he had surprised her. She didn't look aghast or upset, just shocked.

"Um. Maybe. But... It's kind of soon."

He lifted his head. That wasn't a solid no. It was a maybe. Although, it could be an I don't want to turn you down flat, so I'll let you down easy.

"Ask me again?" she said, her hand going out like she was going to put it on his arm, but she drew back just a bit and it landed on the back of the chair instead.

"You can ask me."

Maybe that was disappointment in her eyes. He wasn't sure. It was definitely disappointment in his heart.

Chapter 8

"What do you think?" Sunday asked as her mother leaned over her shoulder, looking at the brochure she had up on her laptop.

"I love the changes you've made. The picture looks like a Hallmark card. I didn't know this old bed-and-breakfast could look like that."

Sunday had spent an entire afternoon trying to get the perfect shot. She did manage to get the charm of the house, along with the big, beautiful shade trees, and even the rope swing off to the side, showcasing the warmth and welcome that guests could feel. Looking at that picture made her heart smile every time.

It was perfect for the front of the brochure.

"I'm so glad Elinor was able to take some time from her dog grooming business and write out your story. If people aren't caught by the picture, they're going to be pulled in by the American dream aspect of everything that you've gone through." She turned around in her chair and put an arm around her mother's waist, leaning her head into her stomach and holding her close.

Sometimes it felt like her mom would live forever, but maybe that was one of the things that she had been learning from Blake's death. She needed to appreciate the people around her while she had them, because everyone had an appointment with death at some point. Even her mother.

Noah.

She hadn't appreciated him when they'd been friends before.

And she turned him down. Why had she turned him down? She tossed and turned over that, although she hadn't thought about it quite as much as she thought about her grief and sorrow.

Still, she regretted it. She wished she would have said yes and they could have set a date two months in the future or something. That would have given her enough time to…what? What did she need time to do?

Her mom said time healed all wounds, but it wasn't even that she needed time to heal. She didn't think she'd burst into tears in the middle of the dinner or anything. And although her appetite hadn't exactly come back, she wasn't feeling sick all the time.

Still, she couldn't hardly change it, although she pulled her phone out of her purse more times than she could count over the last week, holding it in her hand, with her thumbs poised above the screen, wanting to text him and ask him if he wanted to meet at the diner.

Had it been just a casual invitation? He had told her that she could be the one to ask him, but he hadn't said how long he would be willing to say yes.

She was afraid she'd lost her chance.

But she supposed he'd taken the chance to ask to begin with. She should take the chance to ask and see if he was still interested. It seemed only fair that both of them were risking something.

"I'm going to go scrub the bathroom that I missed this morning. I can't believe I forgot it," her mother said as she shook her head and walked away.

Anytime something like that happened with her mom, she worried that maybe her mom was going senile or getting

Alzheimer's. She didn't think so, but it was something that was in her head.

And there she was, worrying again. She needed to rest in the knowledge that God was going to do whatever was best. And if that meant her mom got Alzheimer's, they would have to find a way to deal with it.

Another good thing that came from Blake's death.

It seemed like the good things were piling up. And the bad things... Maybe they weren't getting smaller, but they seemed less impossible to overcome.

Today was the day. She decided that as soon as she was finished with the brochure, she was going to go to her apartment. Maybe she would just be able to step into the candy store. Although, that would be almost as painful as her apartment, since Blake's presence would be everywhere. She put toys behind the counter for him to play with, she ordered a certain kind of candy because he enjoyed it. She made his favorite and displayed it prominently.

She hit print on the brochure and then closed her computer.

Taking the printed brochure from the printer, she folded it. It was smaller than it would be, since the paper was just regular paper, but it was a good representation of what she wanted.

At some point, she would text Noah and let him know that she had the first sample for him when he was ready to view it.

It might be a little awkward talking to him, but she would have to push that aside. Maybe she'd have another chance to apologize. But it didn't bode well for the relationship if she started out every conversation with an apology. She wanted to be better than that.

Sticking the brochure in her purse, she hollered up the stairs to her mom that she was leaving and walked out.

Maybe she could do this. Her stomach revolted, and her feet felt like she was walking through wet cement.

Her chest felt weighted down and heavy, and she almost turned around three times before she was out of the yard and onto the walk.

She turned toward the lake, lifting her eyes to look at its vast blue expanse and remembering that if God could keep the waters of the lake within the shores, He could certainly help her walk a two-block walk to her candy shop.

She thought about stopping at Kristin's. She hadn't talked to her since last week before Noah had shown up. She wanted to find out how Becky and Rita were doing, and she wouldn't mind stopping at the diner and finding out about Rodney too. Last she heard, he was almost ready to start offering rides with the buggy he had specially made to ride in the sand behind his Percherons.

From what she understood, Chi had indicated that he was going to take a gap year, but he'd applied to college for next year.

They were hoping he would stay close, but Chi had confided that she wanted him to do what God wanted him to do and not take her feelings into consideration. So she'd not said anything to him about wanting him to stay.

It was funny how quickly someone could worm their way into a person's heart.

And how devastated a person could be when they were no longer with them.

She tried not to have those negative thoughts in her head, but it was hard.

The breeze blew, lifting her hair from her shoulders, as she walked, slower and slower, down the sidewalk.

Somehow her mouth was dry, and her heart hammered, and she wasn't even sure why. She wasn't afraid. She just...didn't want to face the memories. Didn't want to look at Blake's things and realize he wasn't there anymore. See him in her mind playing with them, hear him calling her name, wishing she had just one more time to tell him she loved him, one more night to tuck him in the bed. She hadn't known that the last night was actually the last night. Maybe she wouldn't have done anything different-ly, other than brand the memory in her head, because she didn't even remem-ber. It had been just another night. Like thousands of nights before and thousands of nights to come. She hadn't realized it would be the last.

Could she live her life like every day was the last?

If she was going to do that, she would have said yes immediately to Noah. He was the kind of man who would be steady and stable.

Although, there was a big gap between when she knew him in high school and seeing him just a week ago. He wasn't married, hadn't been, but that didn't mean he didn't have relationships. Maybe he had a whole string of them and couldn't commit. She would want to know those things before she made any kind of move toward him. Maybe that's why she said no.

She wasn't going to feel guilt about Blake. She wasn't going to blame herself. She was just going to make the best decision she could and move on from there.

Holding tight to her purse with one hand, she walked around the side of the building and put her hand on the doorknob of the back door. She didn't even think she'd locked it. And sure enough, it turned easily under her hand.

Strawberry Sands was not exactly a hotbed of crime, and while normally she would have made sure it was locked, she hadn't even thought about it in the last three weeks.

Taking a breath against the memories she was sure would assail her, she stepped in. Sure enough, the scent was familiar, one she'd always loved, chocolate and sweet and just a hint of disinfectant. She'd always loved the smell of her candy shop.

Interestingly, instead of being overwhelmed by memories, she was overwhelmed by the feeling that she wanted to get back to work. Wanted to start creating new recipes, perfecting the candy she had been working on, and designing creations that tourists could only get in Strawberry Sands.

She'd been hoping for a while that her newest creation, chocolate-covered strawberry buttercream candy, would cause tourists to come back. She'd come up with the strawberry buttercream recipe and had just thought about dipping it in chocolate. White chocolate, milk chocolate, and dark chocolate.

Her fingers itched to get back behind her stove, work out her recipes, and create things that would make people smile.

And contribute to their fun vacation memories.

She stopped; she could hear Blake's voice. Hear his footsteps tripping across the floor, see him coming at her with his arms stretched wide and a big smile on his face. See his impish grin as he asked if he could try it. That he was the candy expert and he could tell her whether it was any good. Of course, that was just his way of getting candy before supper. It was funny, but Sunday was happy for the times where she'd given in and allowed him to have a small piece. Happy for all the times that she'd said yes. She didn't want to spoil her child, and she needed to say no, but it was the yes answers now that made her smile.

Maybe that was another lesson. Saying yes to God. To say yes to the opportunities He gave her. Saying yes to the open doors He put in front of her. Saying yes to trusting Him. Saying yes to holding onto Him as tight as she could and doing her very, very best.

It seemed so easy, but why was it actually so difficult? So difficult to let go of her fears and her anxieties and all the things that she wanted. Why did she think that God was just going to give her pain and heartache? That following Him was going to be worse than choosing her own way?

She started walking down the hall toward the kitchen, and she might have been okay, except as she opened the kitchen door, she looked down, and there, on the floor, were Blake's sneakers. She'd told him three times to take them and put them by the door where they belonged, and he hadn't done it.

And now she remembered, when she put him to bed the last time, she hadn't read him a story because he hadn't put his shoes away.

She sank to her knees and started to cry.

Chapter 9

Dear Business Boy,

I went to my shop today. I haven't gone since Blake... Anyway, I thought I could handle it. After all, I feel so much stronger than I did a week after his funeral. I have my mind headed in the right direction, and I keep thinking about how God has to be in charge of my life. I feel like I've surrendered everything to Him, and then sometimes the pain just becomes so overwhelming that I can't even stand up.

I didn't tell anyone else, but when I went in, I was okay. I even wanted to cook again.

I've been working on different recipes and trying to perfect a strawberry buttercream candy. I'd just decided I needed to cover it in chocolate when Blake...

Everything is before Blake and after Blake.

Anyway, I was excited because I actually wanted to cook. It's the first time that I've really been maybe not excited, but at least looking forward to something. I just...feel hopeless. I surrendered to God, I've given Him everything, but I just don't see any brightness in my future. But that doesn't make sense. It's not that I don't think that God is going to give me good things. I know He will. I know He loves me.

It's just... Maybe it's depression. Whatever, today I just felt a little flicker of...something. I wanted to do something. I wanted to want to, which makes a difference. I haven't wanted to do anything.

So, yeah, I walked into the kitchen, and maybe I would have gotten a few things out. I wasn't planning on cooking, but I could have tried to mix up a batch. Whatever I make, the diner will sell or whatever. But as I walked in, I saw Blake's shoes. I remembered that our last night together hadn't been the best night ever. In fact, I punished him because he hadn't put his shoes away like I told him to do three different times.

He was old enough to listen and obey. And I know, as a parent, rationally I know I need to teach my child that if he doesn't obey, there are consequences. I know that. It just broke my heart that the last night I spent with him was one of punishment and not of joy and happiness.

I cried on the floor for a long time.

I wouldn't tell just anyone, but since you don't feel like someone who's going to see me and judge me, I thought I could tell you.

You are right about someone coming to have Mom make a brochure for the hotel. You must have good contacts. It happened just like you said.

Noah Sterner came, and he brought back some memories too. I'd known him in school, and we were quite good friends. I might have had a little crush on him, but Glenn came in and kind of swept me off my feet.

I wish I would never have allowed that now. Looking back, I was infatuated with everything he represented—adulthood, freedom, money, and fun.

Noah was more of regular life and slightly boring.

I wish I would have gone for slightly boring. My life would be a lot different, I'm sure. Noah is a businessman in Chicago. And I probably wouldn't even live in Strawberry Sands. Which makes me sad. Also, if I hadn't been with Glenn, I wouldn't have had Blake. And even though the pain of the last four weeks has been almost to the point where I don't feel like I can bear it, I wouldn't trade those seven years I had with him.

Not for anything.

Still, one choice can have far-reaching consequences, and I suppose that's another thing I've learned.

So, you know a lot about me, but I don't know much about you. I guess if we're going to continue to write, you should tell me some about yourself.

Sunday sat on her bed and stared at the paper. She wanted to see who he was, what he looked like. Did she dare ask him out to eat with her?

She had turned Noah down, and she regretted that. The businessman seemed nice, and she was just asking as a friend. Maybe she should be clear about that.

She leaned back against her headboard, in her bed back in the attic room at her mother's. She'd managed to get out of the kitchen, close the door and lock it, and walk back to the bed-and-breakfast. She hadn't gone up to her apartment. That was a trip for another day.

She thought a bit before she started to write again.

I suppose you know the diner in Strawberry Sands has a new menu? It's really delicious. One of the features for June is onion soup bread, and you would not believe how amazing it is. I've had it several times, and my mom teases me that I'm going to gain back the weight I've lost when I couldn't eat after Blake's...

I suppose I'll not only gain the weight back but add a few more pounds to it, if I keep eating like that. Still, it's delicious.

Maybe you'd like to meet me there sometime?

Thanks for writing to me. It...has helped.

Your friend,

Lover of the lake

Chapter 10

Noah stood on the ground beside Franklin and stared at the walls of the hotel.

He had been right on when he told Sunday that it would go up fast. It had. In the four weeks since they'd started construction, they had the basement poured, the sides up, and the walls framed out.

He hadn't answered Sunday's last letter. She actually asked Business Boy out to eat, when she refused his invitation.

It had struck him as funny but also made him sad. Once she saw Business Boy was him, she wouldn't be interested anymore.

Of course, it was just as friends, but it didn't matter. She hadn't wanted to go out with Noah himself as just a friend, then she asked someone that she didn't even know.

It bothered him.

"Noah? Did you hear me?" Franklin asked from beside him.

"Sorry. I was thinking."

"Changing your mind about moving in?" The moving truck was supposed to be unloading their things at their apartments above the old diner as they spoke.

When he went "home" tonight, there should be a bed in his apartment, and his electricity and water should be turned on. There was already a stove and refrigerator provided, and in the landing above the stairs was a washer and dryer which Franklin and he would share.

That was really all he needed.

"No. I'm looking forward to it. I told my realtor to make an offer on the property that I looked at on the other side of the house Griff bought. I haven't heard back."

"You're further ahead than I am. I'm not even scheduled to go look at things until next week."

"You need to get a better realtor."

"I like the one I have. She's cute."

"It's more important that she can do her job." Noah rolled his eyes.

"I know. But I want one I'm not afraid to talk to."

Franklin had never met anyone he was afraid to talk to. But Noah just shrugged his shoulders and looked away. Franklin was determined to never get married. He decided that he wasn't the marrying type. Noah wasn't going to argue with that. Franklin knew himself better than anyone, although he kind of figured that God commanded man to marry. He heard people complaining that the earth was overcrowded, but he figured God knew when the earth was full, and He could do something about it.

Until then, man's duty was to obey.

Regardless, it was hardly something that he needed to think about now. It wasn't like he was in any danger of having the woman he wanted want him back.

No. She wanted Business Boy. Someone she'd never even met.

Except she had.

This was a mess.

"Noah? What's up, man?"

It was Franklin again, and once again, he caught Noah not paying attention.

"Sorry. What were you saying?"

"What's the problem?"

"No problem." Other than the fact that he was in some kind of mess that he never even imagined he could possibly be in, and he didn't know what to do about it.

Write her back.

But what was he going to say?

He shoved the thought aside and focused on Franklin and the things they needed to check with the hotel.

He was able to successfully put Sunday out of his head, mostly anyway, until he walked into his apartment that evening.

Franklin and he had parted at their doors. He enjoyed being with his friend but didn't mind going to his own place to be alone.

He wanted to write Sunday back, he just wasn't sure what to say.

After a shower and after he'd heated up the leftovers that he brought home from the diner and had a light supper, he sat down at the kitchen table with his notebook and a pen.

He wanted to talk to her. Was thrilled to have that connection and wanted to keep it. But he wasn't sure if he was ready to meet her. What would she say when she found out Business Boy was him?

Dear Lover of the lake,

It made me sad all over again to hear that you had such a hard time walking into your candy store. The candy store should be a happy place. And I'm sure it was. Thing is, I'm sure it will be again too. You're just that kind of person. I can tell you're not going to let this get you down. That you're going to make this a success. That you're going to allow everything that happened with Blake to inspire you to be better.

That's inspired me.

I wish there was some way I could help you; I wished that from the beginning. Anyway, you asked to know a little more about me, and I guess I really never introduced myself very well. I own my own business, and I partner with a friend on a lot of my investments. I like to be very hands-on, and I have what many might consider an unconventional approach. I went to school for business, but I've had experience in what works and what doesn't.

From what I've learned, businesses work best when the owner is invested. In everything. Of course, I think businesses also work best when the owner realizes his limitations and doesn't try to manipulate things or micromanage things he doesn't really know anything about. I've seen that happen, and I've tried not to do that. Because a man can really get in his own way when he starts to do stuff like that.

I guess I was busy building my business and never really dated seriously, or I suppose more accurately, I don't change my affections very easily, and once I fall for someone, it's hard for me to unfall. Or whatever. Anyway, I haven't dated much, and the dates I've been on have been spectacularly unspectacular. I guess my heart just wasn't in them. I've never had a girl interested enough to accept an offer for a second date, not that I've made that many.

So there, that is the entirety of my dating history. It's pretty boring. Actually, my life isn't that interesting. I'm a pretty calm dude who is content with very little. I've even had people say that I should be more of a go-getter.

I should reach for more. But doesn't the Bible teach us to be content?

So I've never really taken that advice. In business, I take risks, and I enjoy stretching myself, but for my personal life... Unless the girl I'm stuck on ever shows interest in me, I'll probably be alone. I suppose there are worse fates. Like being married to someone who you'd prefer not to be married to. Or worse would be being married to someone who would prefer not to be married to you.

Now that I'm done with the horror stories, I've been thinking about your last question. About going out for lunch sometime.

I think I'd like that. Eventually.

Are you sure you're ready?

Your friend,
Business Boy

A whine made Sunday's head snap up. She hadn't been paying any attention at all as she walked down the sidewalk toward the beach.

But now, the Great Pyrenees that typically hung around town stood in front of her, his tail wagging, his face tilted to the side. His eyes worried.

She'd never thought that a dog could have worried eyes, but this one definitely seemed concerned.

"What's the matter?" she asked, slowing her stride and reaching out to put her hand on the dog's head.

He was a common sight around Strawberry Sands, but as far as she knew, no one owned him and everyone took care of him.

He whined, licked her hands, and then looked off to the side.

He was glancing at the pasture field, and Sunday followed his gaze.

She didn't see anything, but her eyes swept the field again. She didn't know where the horses were, but there weren't any in sight.

Except, the dog whined again, shoved his nose into her hands, and pushed it toward the fence.

"I know. My brother owns that field, but I'm not going to just walk through it. I'm going to stay on the path where I belong." So odd that it seemed like the dog wanted her to go into the pasture field. That was so strange.

Then, she heard something that wasn't quite a whinny but seemed to be some kind of animal sound.

The dog whined again.

Interesting.

And then, movement caught her eye. Just behind a hump in the field, she thought she saw something move.

The dog didn't have to convince her to go over the fence. Sunday had grown up on the farm, and while they didn't have horses back when she was a kid, and she didn't have much experience with them, she'd helped Matt out a few times and had been riding more than once.

She loved it, and so had Blake.

She stumbled a bit at the thought of her son, but the sound came again and she hurried on.

As she got closer to the hump, she could see better and realized that there was a horse lying on its side. One foot stuck out of its rear end, making it obvious it was in labor.

Immediately, she grabbed for her phone and found her brother Matt's contact.

She called him, even as she walked slowly closer to the mare. Matt didn't have any horses that were exceptionally wild, so she talked softly, coming around to the mare's head and touching her wide forehead.

The mare seemed to be in distress and also seemed to be exhausted.

"Hello?"

"Matt. You need to come out to the side field right away. You have a mare out here who's having a baby. And she's in some kind of trouble. I only see one leg."

"Be right out." Matt hung up, and she swiped off as well.

When they had the farm, she'd helped deliver more than a few calves, but horses were different, and she didn't know what to do. With a calf, she knew they needed to have two hooves.

The mare didn't seem to notice when she left her head and walked back to take another look.

Still just one foot. The mare seemed to be straining, and Sunday wanted to help but didn't know what to do.

Upon closer inspection, she realized the mare looked skinny and seemed to be in rather bad shape.

Matt never let his horses get run down like that, and she wondered what was going on with this one.

She heard the four-wheeler before she saw it careen over the crest of the hill.

Matt slowed down before he got to her, stopping some distance away, most likely so he wouldn't scare the horse. He had a bucket of water with a lid on it and a few other things that he grabbed as he jumped off the four-wheeler.

"I called the vet, but she's on call with someone else. What's up?" he asked as he got closer.

"I told you. Just one leg. She seems to be straining, and she looks exhausted."

"I got her from the kill pen and was told she wasn't due for another three months. I just put her out here by herself, because she needed so much conditioning. I figured when she had her foal, it would need to be supplemented. But I wasn't expecting it to come today."

Matt spoke as he moved around her back, then set the water down, and used a disinfectant wipe he had with him to wipe his hands and arms. "I might need you. My arms might be too big."

"Me?" Sunday said, although she heard him well enough. It had been years since she'd done anything of the sort.

He didn't bother to answer her but grunted as he ran a hand down the horse's rump and used his other hand to carefully work his way down the leg sticking out to see if he could find the second leg.

"I need you," he said simply.

Sunday didn't question him, but grabbed a wipe, and wiped her arms and hands.

If it meant saving a life, she'd do it. She removed everything else from her head and focused on what Matt was telling her about feeling for the second leg and possibly needing to straighten it out. Telling her to make sure she felt the nose and that the foal was in the same position a cow should be as he came down the birth canal.

She heard him and did her best. The inside of the birth canal was wet and warm, and Sunday could easily feel her way up the leg they could see sticking out.

But as she made it halfway up, she could feel the second leg, twisted back.

"I'm going to have to straighten the second leg," she said, carefully feeling to see if it was just twisted or completely bent around.

"I think you need to do it quickly, no pressure," Matt said, and it was her turn to grunt.

She couldn't work any faster.

"I think I'm going to need two hands."

"That's what I thought too," Matt said.

They worked in silence for a bit, with her working by feel and Matt attempting to hold the tail away, stroking the horse's side, trying to keep her calm.

He mentioned a few things that the vet had said, advice that she'd given, and he also said just before he hung up the vet had warned him that they might have to make a choice between saving the mare and saving the foal.

"Which are we going to do if it comes to that?" Sunday asked.

"I guess it will depend on the situation," Matt said grimly. "My ideal would be to save them both. That's the goal."

Sunday nodded. She had been able to get both of her hands on the foal's twisted leg and gently push it back until she was able to straighten it out.

"I got it!" she said, excitement in her voice, but she kept it down so she didn't scare the mare.

"Hey, guys, is everything okay?"

She turned, both hands still reaching around trying to find the foal's head, but her eyes went to the man who just walked around the knob and was striding toward them.

Noah.

"Hey, man. We could use some help."

"All right." He sounded unsure. "This isn't exactly my thing, but I'm a quick learner." Noah stopped beside her.

"Do me a favor and go up and sit by her head. She's been calm this whole time, but we need her to stay down so we can get this baby out."

"All right." Noah spoke to Matt, but his eyes were on her. There might have been a glimmer of humor in his eyes at her position, but there was also a deep concern.

Noah had always been kind of a sensitive guy like that. Back when they had been friends, he'd always been concerned about other people's pain.

It made sense that he would love animals too. Although she honestly didn't know.

"I feel the head, I think." Her fingers touched something soft. "I think it's an ear."

"You might need to move the head around. It might be twisted back."

She didn't say anything for a moment while her fingers tried to feel down to the base of the ear and then figure out the direction of the head.

The mare pushed, and the birth canal tightened around her hands.

She would much rather the vet be there. She didn't know whether she was doing this right or not, whether the mare would survive or not, whether the foal was already gone. But in the absence of the vet, all they could do was their best.

Time was of the essence.

"I feel its nose."

"You might have to stick your fingers in it, to get purchase on the head. The vet had mentioned something about that."

"All right." Her arms felt like jelly, from the pressure she pushed against, and her thighs ached because of the unfamiliar position. She realized her back hurt as well.

She tried to stop thinking about all the things that were feeling terrible and tried to focus on the fact that if they could save this foal, she would be smiling the rest of the day. And well into the next. Probably into the next week.

The mare pushed again, and she waited until the contraction had ended before she put both hands on the legs and pushed backward far enough that she could get the head turned into position.

It took her three more tries and two more contractions until she felt she had it ready.

"I think that's the best I can do." She slid her hands out and sat back on her haunches.

Noah stared at her, and she met his eyes, still concerned about the horse and her baby but also feeling...something...for the man holding her head.

He hadn't hesitated when they'd said they needed help.

"How did you know we were back here?" she asked as the horse pushed again, and she looked down.

"There was a dog on the sidewalk. A white one. I've seen it around town a lot but don't know whose it is. He wouldn't let me pass. He just kept pushing me in this direction until I finally heard something. I'm not even sure what it was."

"I heard her trying to whinny, but it came out as a strangled, painful sigh."

He laughed. "That's exactly what it sounded like."

"There's a nose!" Matt said, drawing Sunday's eyes back down to the foal. "The vet said sometimes when they're not in position, that means they died in utero."

His words hung in the air. Sunday's heart sank down to her toes. Had she just done all of that work only to deliver a dead baby?

She supposed it needed to come out, to save the life of the mare. Still, she didn't want another dead baby. She wanted a live one.

Then she remembered, it wasn't about what she wanted.

Lord, if You would, let it be born alive.

It was God's choice. But she could let Him know what she wanted and pray for that end.

So that's exactly what she did.

"A few more good pushes and we should have the head out," Matt said, shifting around so he was in a better position to give her a hand.

It turned out he didn't need to, because less than a minute later, the foal slipped out, small and wet and still. After a few seconds while Sunday held her breath, its chest trembled, and its head lifted, its eyes wide open.

"It's alive!" she breathed, her hand going to her chest.

Matt produced a rag from somewhere, and he wiped the mucus out of its airways. "It sure is." He stopped for a moment and looked up at her, smiling. "You did a good job."

"I can't believe it's alive."

Sunday looked over in surprise. Noah stood beside her, and his hand came down on her shoulder. "I'm not sure I could have done that. I...was shocked that you were able to."

"I was shocked too. I haven't done anything close to that in years. And never with a horse."

"Do you think the mom is going to make it?"

Chapter 12

Matt shrugged his shoulder and leaned back, allowing the foal to struggle to get up off its side. "I'm not sure. The vet's coming, and we'll do what we can for her. I'm almost positive the baby is going to need to be supplemented though."

"You mean like with a bottle?" Noah asked.

"Kinda. Probably with a bucket. Foals can drink from a very young age; she probably won't drink from a bottle if she's getting anything from her mom."

"That'll probably have to happen pretty often, won't it?" Noah asked as Matt handed the rag to Sunday and she found a dry spot with which to wipe off her arms.

"I think every two to three hours. I'm sure the vet will know better when she gets here, but that reminds me. Sunday, Jubilee and the kids and I had a trip planned the day after tomorrow. Just a day trip, but a little family time since the kids are out of school, before we get super busy at the stables. If we still go on that, do you think you can feed this little guy?"

"Um…" Somehow her eyes met Noah's.

"I'll help you." He grinned.

"I think you like this."

"Maybe. I might have been born to be a farmer and just didn't realize it."

"If you were born to be a farmer, you were at the wrong end."

"I'm pretty sure I was at the right end." He grinned again. Sunday couldn't help smiling with him. Maybe partly out of relief that the baby was okay, although she was still worried about the mom. And partly because Noah was gently teasing her, and she liked it.

"All right. Sounds like Noah and I will give you a hand if you need it. Just give us very detailed instructions, because I don't want to mess anything up."

"All right."

"If you don't mind, I told Mom that I was just taking a short walk, and I want to head back up. So I'm not going to wait for the vet with you, but I'd really like to know what she says."

"Go on ahead. I'll be waiting for the vet, and we'll go from there."

"I wouldn't mind an update, too, once you find out what she says," Noah said, and Matt nodded.

"I'll text you both."

"Thanks."

As she moved away, Noah fell into step beside her, and they walked around the little hump and toward the fence.

"I wouldn't have known about it if that dog hadn't helped me," Sunday said, trying to sound casual, although she was very aware of the man beside her.

"Same. I had no idea you two were back there."

"It feels like he's a pretty smart animal."

"I think Great Pyrenees were bred to protect their flocks and herds. He was probably just doing what instinct demanded he do."

"Do you think?" She wanted to believe that the dog was extremely intelligent. Maybe an alien in disguise. Or maybe just a guardian angel.

But Noah's expLenation sounded much more feasible than hers did.

"I guess we'll never know. There's no way to tell."

"True," she said as they reached the fence and she put a foot on the bottom rung, swinging a leg over and dropping down on the other side.

She waited for Noah while he did the same.

"That was a pretty amazing experience," he said.

"I never get tired of seeing animals be born. I agree. It was incredible."

"And so are you. I mean that."

She shook her head. "No. I think if Matt weren't there, I would have panicked. I didn't do anything until he came and started ordering me around. That's what

I needed. Someone in there telling me what to do."

"That's half the battle, I think. I mean, someone needs to know what to do, and someone needs to be able to do it."

"I guess that makes sense."

"Anyway. I'll never forget that. It was pretty amazing."

She had to agree. And she probably could add that it was even more amazing that she got to share it with him. But she wasn't sure why she wanted to say that. So she didn't.

"What were you doing?" she asked as they started back up the sidewalk.

"I saw you walking down and thought I'd follow you."

"Are you serious?" she said, laughter in her voice. She thought he was joking. Why would he be following her?

"Yeah. I was done for the day and saw you walking by." He shrugged. "I wasn't stalking you or anything, so don't even think that."

"I wasn't. I was just surprised." Then she sobered as they drew closer to her candy store. "I told Mom I was going to walk on the beach, but I actually was thinking about stopping at the candy store and trying to go in my apartment. I still haven't made it."

"We can do that if you want to. Do you think it'll go better if I'm with you?"

She hadn't considered taking people in with her before, but she hadn't really wanted to. She wasn't sure why, whether it was just something that she felt like she needed to do on her own, or whether she was afraid to have anyone with her in case she couldn't handle it.

"No pressure, if you'd rather not." Noah said, and she appreciated the fact that he wasn't pushing her.

"You might see the worst side of me," she said, lifting a brow at him and biting both of her lips.

That made both sides of his mouth curve up. She hadn't meant to have that reaction at all. "I'm not afraid."

She snorted. "Maybe you should be."

"I doubt it. We all have that side. That side we really don't want anyone else to see. I suppose, I understand, but I'm also fine. Because I know that we all have it."

"All right." She pursed her lips, moving forward, and then she took a breath and slid her hand into his.

Looking up, she said, "Do you mind?"

He squeezed her hand and shook his head, a smile tripping over his lips.

"Do you want me to go first?" he asked as they walked back between the buildings, and she dug the key to her door out of her pocket.

"No. I can do it. I'm prepared to see the shoes in the kitchen."

"The shoes?" he said. Then she realized that she had never told him about the shoes. That had been Business Boy.

What did it say about her that she got Noah and Business Boy confused?

She didn't want to have to explain it to him, didn't want to go down that trail if she didn't have to, not as she did something as hard as walking in. She just opened the door, shoved the key back in her pocket, and held on tight to Noah's hand as she walked in.

He wasn't going to let her go, and she appreciated that.

She pushed open the door to the kitchen, saw the shoes, and this time, she smiled at them.

She had good memories with her son. And now she had a life without him. And God had orchestrated both.

And somehow God orchestrated the fact that this man had once been in her life, and now he was again. She'd taken a detour, gone off with Glenn, had the best thing that ever happened to her in Blake, and now God had given her... Maybe not another chance with Noah, but at least a chance to be friends with him. And she would take it.

"It smells amazing in here." Noah sniffed deeply.

"The smell has always made me smile. Just candy and sweetness and it smells clean too."

"Exactly. Smells like happiness. Like the way I'd want my trip to the beach to smell if I took one."

"That's what I'm hoping for. To help people make good memories on their vacation. Of course, I'd like to make money while I'm doing it, but that's the goal anyway."

He nodded, looking around the kitchen, and then he looked back at her, searching her face as though checking for any signs that she was in distress. "Are you handling this okay?"

She realized she was. She nodded. "Thank you for coming. I don't know if that made the difference, or if I'm just finally ready."

He nodded, holding tight to her hand and allowing her to lead him as she walked through the kitchen, touching one of her copper pots, running her hand along her butcher block counter, feeling the cold smoothness of the granite countertop she had installed along the side.

She walked to the counter where the wall opened as a window to the small storefront. She could be in the kitchen and look out.

She'd missed this. And she had a deep longing to get back to it.

But she felt like she needed to conquer her apartment first.

"Do you mind going upstairs with me?" she asked, and there was a tremble in her voice. She didn't really want to. But each time she did it, it would get easier.

"I don't mind at all. Lead the way."

"All right."

As they stepped out of the kitchen, she picked up Blake's shoes with her free hand.

Going down the hall, she set them in front of the door where they belonged.

She supposed that would be one of the last motherly things she ever did. At least that she ever did for Blake. Putting his shoes away for him.

Such a simple thing. But she refused to feel guilty for punishing him for not listening. It was important that he learned. She'd had no idea that he was going to die the next day. She had to be the best mother she could be, and that included making sure her child learned to listen.

Of course, if she were able to see the future, she would have done things differently, but since she wasn't, she couldn't. And that was the way it was supposed to be. That was the way God ordained it; she didn't get a say. She had to accept it. And she did. Her choice was whether or not she would accept it. And she chose to do so. God was right.

Holding tight to Noah's hand, she put first one foot and then another on the steps, until she reached the top, opening up the door and stepping in.

Immediately a sense of home surrounded her, and she put a hand on her stomach.

"Are you okay?" Noah asked from behind her. He took one step closer and stood with her back touching his chest.

"Yeah. Just give me a minute," she said, her voice weak.

He slid his hand over her arm, until his hand covered hers, and he pulled her snug against him. Not so tight she couldn't breathe. Not so tight she felt trapped. Just tight enough to know that she wasn't alone, and that he was there for her. It was the perfect amount of pressure, and she leaned into him, grateful for his presence and for his concern and compassion. For his care, for his caring.

The kitchen was exactly the way she had left it; she'd washed the dishes before they'd gone for their walk that day, but she hadn't dried them or put them away, and they were still in the draining board. Just like she'd left them.

Their coats hung on the rack by the door, and Blake's favorite cereal sat on the counter.

The box was too big to fit in the cupboard, and that was the only place she could keep it. Other than the top of the refrigerator.

Her eyes fell on it, and she saw the latest paper that he brought home from school held up on the refrigerator with magnets. Their Christmas card with a picture of the two of them was on it as well.

She supposed the bedroom would be the hardest part, but she took another step into the kitchen, and Noah let her go. Her back felt cold as she stepped away from him, but she held on tightly to his hand, and he followed her.

"I can do this. It hurts, and I'm a little scared, and I feel a lot of pain, but I can do it." She was talking to herself just as much as she was talking to him.

"Of course you can do it. You have to. You're facing it, and you're moving forward. Not forgetting, just knowing that this is the life you have."

"Right. This is the life I have, and it's a good one."

It was the truth, and it was encouraging to remember that. It might not be exactly what she wanted, but it was a good life. And she had so much to be thankful for.

And she had all of the memories. They were good memories. And she wouldn't want to not have them.

"You know, you don't have to do anything to his room right now," Noah said as she started in the direction of the bedrooms.

"I know. I thought about shutting the door and not thinking about it. Do you think that it will get easier to open it after some time has passed?"

Her mother said time healed all wounds. It made things easier. Would next year this time be just as hard?

"I think the first time is always going to be hard. No matter when it is. But, just guessing here, because I have no experience, I'd say that the longer you wait, the easier the first time will be."

She nodded. Looking down the hall, she saw his door was closed.

"Then I think I'll wait." She didn't think she was taking the coward's way out. She was making a decision based on facts. It was a fact that she'd already done a lot today, and probably doing more wasn't a smart idea. It was a fact that time did make things easier. It eased the pain, blurred the memories, and she would have time between to make new memories. To realize that her life could be full, even though she would always miss her son.

"Thanks for doing this with me," she said.

"My pleasure. Do you think you're going to stay with your mom?" he asked as she turned and didn't go into her bedroom either. That would be hard. But she didn't really need to. She could grab some more clothes, but she'd managed to live this long with what she had, so it wouldn't be a problem to continue.

"No. I don't think so," she said, lifting her chin, although her words were thoughtful and not determined. "I think I'm going to open my candy shop again. Mom has been gracious to me, letting me hang out there, but I think I'm ready to start back out on my own two feet."

"A month and a half isn't a very long time to grieve. Not for something like this."

"Really? It feels like I've been in this pit for a really long time. Feels like it's more than past time for me to get out and join the living again."

"I'm not an expert, but this feels like one of those things that different people take different times for. I think the important thing is keeping your mindset in the right direction and not allowing yourself to get bitter and angry, either at God, or yourself, or anything else. And you've done that beautifully."

She smiled and looked up at him, suddenly very aware of their joined hands and their close proximity.

"I appreciate the compliments, but I appreciate even more the fact that you were here with me." Her smile widened. She had a letter to write, but she also had a man in front of her who was solid and strong and dependable. And was willing to be patient with her when she needed it. Willing to be with her when she just needed a body, someone warm and strong to lean on.

It's what she'd always wanted in a man. It's what Glenn never was and what Noah was naturally.

She had been foolish when she was younger.

Chapter 13

Dear Business Boy,

I think I'm ready. I'm ready to... I hate to say move on, although that's kind of what it is. But I'm ready to start living again. Holding the memories close, of course. I don't ever want to feel like Blake wasn't an important part of my life. And I'll always look forward to getting to heaven and seeing him. But in the meantime, it's important that I start doing what God wants me to do. Your letters have been a life-saver at a time when my life seemed rather hopeless.

Maybe they didn't exactly give me hope, but they gave me a glimmer of something. Hope seems as good a word as any to describe it.

My life seems like it's filled with hope now. Hope for the future, hope for my business, hope for everything. And yes, I'd like to meet you.

How about we do this: I make candy for a living. At least I used to. I'm planning on doing it again. How about you go to the diner and sit at a table with a bag of candy on the edge. That way, when I arrive, I'll know who you are. Does that sound okay?

I don't know how old you are, what you look like, or anything. I'm kind of curious, but I don't want you to tell me now. I'll just meet you when I meet you.
Does that sound good?
Your appreciative friend,
Lover of the lake

Dear Lover of the Lake,
That sounds perfect to me. But you forgot to tell me what day. I have to be away for a bit, so how about we do it

the third Tuesday of next month? It'll
be the day after I get back.
If that doesn't suit, let me know, other-
wise you can expect to see me there.
With candy.
Your friend,
Business Boy

Chapter 14

Noah stood on the front step of the bed-and-breakfast waiting for Sunday to come out.

It was early, six o'clock, and Sunday had said she would slip out as soon as she could, but she needed to help her mom with breakfast prep first.

Rather than going in, he had told her he would wait outside. It seemed like if there were guests milling around inside, one more person would just add to the melee.

Plus, he enjoyed the view of the lake from the porch.

There was just something soothing about that spot, a cozy, small-town feeling that descended on him when he was in Strawberry Sands. The bed-and-breakfast, with good smells of bacon and toast wafting out, only added to that feeling.

The whole area just felt like home to him.

He had been disappointed there hadn't been a house for sale in town. He loved the property he had made an offer on outside of Strawberry Sands, and the view of the lake from the bluff was amazing, but he loved the town. Loved being in it, loved the feeling he got as he sat on the front step of the bed-and-breakfast and enjoyed the view.

A thought came into his head as he sat there. Would Lena be interested in selling?

He almost snorted. There he was building a hotel and thinking about buying a bed-and-breakfast?

Sunday really seemed to enjoy working there, and she could have her candy shop in the bed-and-breakfast. That might help with sales.

Would he live there? What would happen to Lena?

He could just see Franklin rolling his eyes, because this was just the type of thing that Noah might do. He was always thinking outside the box, making things work that no one else had thought of, not afraid to try.

"Good morning!" Sunday opened the door and stepped out, sounding a little breathless. "Have you been waiting long?"

He rose, looking at her, fresh faced, with rosy cheeks and sparkling eyes. She still wore an apron over her T-shirt and jeans, and her pink painted toenails stuck out from her flip-flops.

"Nope. Busy morning?" he said, wanting to walk to her and put his arms around her but knowing they didn't really have that kind of relationship. Not yet, anyway.

"Oh my goodness. Two families with small children; it was crazy. Usually we just have couples." She laughed a little. "Those are probably the people who will stay at the hotel once it's built."

"Yeah." He wanted to ask her about that. But first, "You're looking really good today."

"Thanks. I... I'm feeling a lot better." She nodded her head, her eyes moving to the side like her thoughts were going inward, like she hadn't thought to check on herself today yet. "I guess... I guess staying busy is the best way. Even though what I want to do is stay in bed."

"I think sometimes we just need to give ourselves a little bit of time to stay in bed. To let the pain subside. But it looks to me like you're doing a lot better now that you're up and about."

"I have to agree with you. I don't think I could have been up those first few days especially, maybe the first week or two. But now... Now I know I feel better if I'm busy looking for things to do, and it always feels good to help Mom. I love working with her."

"And why is that?" he asked, truly curious. It wasn't often that people had great relationships with their parents. He never really did.

"I don't know. She's just...chill. She doesn't get upset about stuff. And it doesn't matter how early we have to get up, she's always in a good mood. I guess maybe she taught me that. Because what's the point in making everyone around you miserable? So you just make yourself smile and be happy." She grinned. "Most of the time." Her face clouded just a little as though she were remembering that maybe she couldn't force herself to be happy after she'd lost her child. But her face brightened again, like she pushed those thoughts aside.

"Are you ready?" he asked, nodding toward the steps.

"I sure am! I'm looking forward to it."

"Me too." And he found that to be true. They stepped off the porch together. "I've not spent much time with animals, but I found myself thinking about how you helped deliver that foal. For some reason, my mind keeps going back to it over and over again, and it just makes me smile."

It wasn't the type of thing that he normally talked to people about, but maybe part of the reason that his mind kept going back to it was because of Sunday, and how much he enjoyed watching her, maybe having just a little part in what she was doing. That probably made him feel just as good as saving the foal.

"I was so scared we were going to lose it." She sighed. "When Matt showed me what to do to feed it yesterday evening, it was so nice to see her up and healthy."

Her face fell. "I guess I didn't tell you that he lost the mare."

A shock went through Noah at the words. "No. I didn't realize."

"Yeah. I hated to bother you with bad news last night. Matt hadn't told me either. I think he was afraid it would..."

"Set you back?" he asked gently, when her words trailed off and she didn't try to continue to talk.

"Yeah. I guess. I hate that everyone feels like they need to treat me with kid gloves now. Like, you know I'm getting better. And I want people to see that. And not be afraid that if they look at me wrong, I'm going to spiral back down into some kind of deep depression and not be able to get out of bed for a week."

"That's because people care about you. They don't want to see anything bad happen to you, so that's why they're being so careful."

"I know. I do know that, and I appreciate it. I... I didn't realize how many people cared about me until this happened."

"Another good thing?" he asked, knowing that she'd been keeping track of all the good things that had come out of what had originally been only a tragedy to her.

"Yes. Another good thing. I see how people care and how they really want to help. How they'll...do whatever they can to try to make you feel better."

He wondered if she was thinking about the letters he had been sending. In one of the first ones, he told her that he didn't know what to do, so he sent her a letter. Maybe other people had done the same thing. He had never even considered that she might be writing to multiple people. For her sake, he hoped so, but for his, it made him a little bit sad. He wanted to be special, not one of many.

Still, he wanted what was best for Sunday. What made her feel better.

Tempted to ask but not wanting her to get suspicious about him possibly being one of her pen pals, he moved to a subject he had wanted to discuss with her. "Do you think your mom might be interested in selling the bed-and-breakfast?"

Her head jerked back as she snapped it around to look at him.

"I'd never considered it," she said with a little bit of wonder in her voice, like she couldn't believe she hadn't. Or maybe she was just surprised that he'd even thought of it.

"I just now thought of it. I was sitting on the porch this morning, and it's so beautiful there. So relaxing and peaceful. It just feels like the cares of the world are somewhere far away when you're sitting on that front porch."

"It's a magical place, isn't it? I don't know how Mom does it. She makes it feel homey, but it's functional at the same time. I mean, she doesn't have knick-knacks or other things stuck everywhere that you're tripping over. It's spacious and clutter free, but still welcoming and warm."

"She definitely has a knack for that. The inside of the bed-and-breakfast is the same."

"And so are the rooms. She just... Just is able to make everything look beautiful wherever she goes, but without a whole lot of fuss. That's Mom. No fuss."

"She has the right atmosphere going. And I don't know, it wasn't that I was looking for a bed-and-breakfast to invest in, I just thought that might be a good place for your candy store too."

"The bed-and-breakfast?" Sunday said, surprise heavy in her voice.

"Sure. There is a kitchen there, you'd be available anytime your guests need-ed you, and you could have your candy on display. Everyone would see it and hopefully talk about it. It would draw people to the bed-and-breakfast, and it would give them something to buy while they're there. You could probably even offer gift samples on their bed in their room when they check in."

"Oh my goodness. All kinds of ideas I've never even thought of. Those are awe-some."

"Yeah, I guess that's just the way my mind works. Always thinking about how you can leverage what you have to make a living on it. So many people are stuck for years in jobs that they hate, and I don't know, I just think about the things that I love and try to think about how I can make a living doing them."

"That's so smart. I mean, this is more than just putting out a product that is good. It's about marketing it too. About reaching people. Although, it seems kind of cold-blooded just to try to sell it to them. You want to...be a blessing to them somehow."

"That's exactly what we were thinking about with the hotel. We wanted to be a complement to Strawberry Sands. I think things like that fit in with the community better. Where it's not cold, hard cash and all about profit, but it's about the community. And sometimes you sacrifice profit in order to do that, but it feeds your soul that way, and it's not a soul-sucking job, but a job that makes you happy, one that makes you feel good about doing good in the world."

"Yeah, I can see how that kind of turns business models on their side. Where, maybe you could make more money, but that's not the only goal."

"Yeah. Franklin is used to me thinking along those lines and coming up with things a little outside of the box. I think most investors thought Strawberry Sands was too small to invest in. Maybe they're right. Maybe we'll never turn a profit on the hotel. But it's a beautiful place, and I think it's unique because of the horses. There isn't much of that along the shores of Lake Michigan."

"The winters are pretty harsh. Michigan can be an unforgiving state at times. You have to be tough to survive here."

"But it's beautiful. Sometimes the things that are hard or maybe difficult destinations are the most beautiful ones as well. And there are plenty of people who are willing to suffer a little, or at least go on an adventure, in order to experience the beauty of their destination."

"You would know that more than me. I just know I love it here."

By that time, they'd gone down to the beach and walked around the pasture to get to the barn.

"We're right on time. He said seven o'clock should be the first feeding, and then we're supposed to do it every three hours after." She bit her lip. "It's okay if you can't make it every time. I actually thought I might stay here and maybe take a ride."

"I have the entire day."

He wanted to spend as much time as he could with Sunday. But he didn't want her to question that too much. Just knew that he enjoyed her company, and that sometimes when he liked a person from afar, getting to know them was more eye-opening about the things that he missed and maybe didn't like so much. But the more time he spent with Sunday, the more he enjoyed spending time with her, and the more he wanted to spend with her.

"If you have an entire day off, you don't have to spend it all here. Or with me." She lifted her brows, and he shook his head.

"I don't want to sound like a stalker, but I can't think of anywhere else I'd rather be than with you."

Chapter 15

Sunday's mouth dropped open in an "O," and she might have said something, except they reached the stable and a whinny shattered the air, shrill and high.

"I think that's our girl."

"It was a girl?"

"Yes," she said as she opened the door and stood back so he could go in.

It was supposed to be the other way around, but he hadn't had any idea of how to open the stable door. It didn't have a doorknob like a normal door.

He made a note for next time. Plus, he hadn't been sure where the foal was.

She came in behind him, shut the door which made it dark inside, and he stood, waiting.

"I'll grab the lights," she said as she walked over. He heard the click just before the lights came on. "She's in the first stall on the left. I'm going to run over and check on her, then go back to the tack room and make the formula."

"I thought she'd be out in the pasture where she was born," he murmured as he followed Sunday as she walked to the stall.

"Matt wanted to keep her in the stall for a while until he was sure she would come to us in the pasture. Trying to catch her might be a little bit difficult. He didn't think it would take very long, and honestly if he were here today, he might have left her out. But he didn't want to make things harder on me."

"That was considerate of him." Sunday had a great family, and he loved how close they were. It made it all the more obvious his lack of family. Of course, Franklin was like a brother to him. And he loved Franklin's brother Peter almost as much.

Still, what would it have been like to grow up with such a close-knit family?

"I admire your family. You guys are all so close."

"That's probably because of my mom. Or maybe even because my dad left." The foal stuck her head over the side of the stall, and Sunday held her hand up while the foal sniffed it. "I guess that's another example of something bad, or at least something that everyone would think was bad, happening, but good came out of it."

"Interesting."

"Yeah. We all had to work together. I mean, Mom didn't make a big deal about it. Sometimes it didn't even feel like I have a dad. She just didn't mention him.

She didn't go around complaining about him or whining that he wasn't paying her, which we found out later that he wasn't, or that she had so much work to do, or that she was scared or anything. It was like she just put her hand in God's hand and then made everything so much fun that my siblings and I just followed along, thinking everything was a big game almost."

"She's quite a woman," Noah said, thinking that Sunday was quite a woman as well.

"I'm thinking of her example more and more as I've been going through the grieving process. For lack of a better word. I see how my mom handled things. I mean, it's not like she lost a child. It's a completely different thing. But it's a devastation nonetheless. And... I'm sure she probably felt like hiding under the bed or lying there with her covers pulled up over her head, but she couldn't. You know?"

"Because she had a bunch of kids to take care of. And you can't just take off."

"Exactly. So yeah, she kept going, but it's more about how she did it. She did it with a smile. With joy, with faith in God. It's like she put her hope in Jesus and never lost that."

"Because when life feels hopeless, what's the point of going on?"

"Yeah. What's the point when you have no hope for anything better?"

Her fingers trailed over the foal's forehead, and the little animal stood on trembling legs, legs that looked way too long for her body, as Sunday spoke softly to her, moving her fingers over her head and down her neck, finding a spot to scratch that made the foal tilt her head to the side and stretch her neck out.

"That's a good spot," he murmured.

"They all have one. You just have to find it."

"People too, probably."

"It's true for a lot of things, I think. Not just physical spots, but we all have those words that we need to hear or things that make us happy or upset us. Like the front porch on the bed-and-breakfast.

How you like that. Some people don't even notice it."

"I don't understand how they couldn't."

"Exactly. And if it isn't her sweet spot that I'm scratching, it doesn't do nearly as much good as it does when I find the right one."

"Yeah. I can see that."

Sometimes animals taught them so much about life, and maybe that's why Scripture had so much about the natural world in it. A lot about sowing and reaping, but God often used animals and other things as analogies in the Bible.

"Can I pet her?" he asked, and Sunday stepped back immediately.

"I think it would be good for her. She needs to learn that people are her friends. Especially since she doesn't have a mom."

"That's sad."

"Yeah." Her voice sounded a little sad, and he wondered if she was thinking about Blake and how she had lost him.

"Maybe you two are meant for each other."

"That's funny. When I was here yesterday, Matt suggested that I take her on as my special project. He even told me I could name her, which is a big deal because he and Jubilee have three girls, and they were all clamoring to be able to name her."

"What did you decide?"

"I'm not sure. I guess if it were a boy, maybe I'd name him Blake. Except... That doesn't feel right. But you know, names aside, I was just thinking about how she doesn't have a mom, and I don't have a son anymore. God didn't drop another baby in my lap, but he gave me a foal to love for now. I mean, she'll be a grown horse someday, and I'm sure Matt has plans for her, but just for a little while, God gave me something to kind of not feel the hole Blake's passing left, but something to focus on and to love."

He loved the way she was looking at that. Like she was looking for the ways that proved God was good.

So often, he found it to be true that whatever a person looked for was what they found. Maybe that was why the Bible commanded them to focus on the things that were good. Whatsoever things are pure, whatsoever things are lovely, whatsoever things are of good report.

"It seems like you're always finding the good in God."

"That's because God is good."

"I suppose there are people who think He's not."

"I guess they'll find out someday that they were wrong, won't they?" She didn't seem like she was interested in arguing with them or in trying to talk them into anything. Maybe that was the best way. God never commanded anyone to argue. And Jesus never did. He just presented the truth, and then people had a choice.

Maybe that's where Christians went wrong sometimes. They wanted to argue and debate. They wanted to talk people into things, when it really wasn't their job to talk people into anything. It was God who touched their hearts or convicted them that they needed something, and it was just man's job to show them the way. And point them to Jesus.

"The command is to go. Go ye into all the world and preach the gospel."

"Exactly. It doesn't say anything about arguing with people."

"No. It doesn't. But it does say that Jesus himself says that they'll know we are Christians by our love. Sometimes I think everyone has it all backward, including me. I certainly haven't been the greatest at showing love."

"Or not arguing. I like to do that. It's kind of fun."

They laughed a little together, and he figured they were in agreement on that.

"All right, let's go to the tack room, and I'll show you how to mix this up. That's if you want to know."

"I'd like to know everything. I'm here. I might as well be put to work."

"You might regret saying that. Sometimes when you're on the farm, you get sucked into the strangest things." She laughed. "I remember one time when we had guests at the bed-and-breakfast, and the cows got out. Mom had all of the guests in the yard, plugging the holes in the fence and chasing the cows out of the garden. It was...quite an experience for them, I'm sure. Several of them said they'd never had so much fun, but there were a couple who didn't have much to say."

"Well, it wasn't like you held a gun to their head and forced them to do it."

"No, but they weren't getting breakfast until Mom got the cows back in, so you know..."

He laughed. "Holding their breakfast hostage is pretty serious stuff."

"Right? Who needs a gun?"

They laughed.

She showed him where the bucket of milk replacer was and scooped out the correct amount, putting it in the bottle.

"Eventually it won't have to be warm, but I like to make it warm because they drink it better that way."

"But not too hot."

"No. Just like a baby. Too hot, it will burn them, although when we're feeding such a small amount, I might make it slightly warmer than I normally might, because it will lose some heat between here and her stall. And I don't want it to be cold."

"That makes sense. There's a lot of surface area for the heat to leak out."

"That's right." She filled up the container with water, used a whisk to stir it, and poured it into the bucket. "Eventually we can eyeball it and not have to measure it. But I haven't done it enough to feel like I can just put the exact right amount of water in. That's why I put it in that container to measure it first."

He nodded, thinking that Sunday felt a lot more at home in the barn than what he expected. But it made sense that she had grown up on a farm. He had a tendency to forget that, since the bed-and-breakfast seemed to be the main business she was involved in, along with the candy store. Before that, she'd moved away entirely, with Glenn.

Still, every interaction with her made him want to be with her more.

Chapter 16

Sunday walked with the bucket toward the foal, very aware of Noah walking beside her.

He had been attentive and sweet, interested and helpful. He seemed to understand that her grief was still there, even though she was trying to push past it and focus on the good.

He helped her to do that while still acknowledging that it was hard for her.

She felt like...like he understood, even though he really couldn't. He had never been through it. But it was like he was trying to understand and not just telling her to snap out of it. She had a few comments like that, not many, but people who thought that she was taking too long to get back to normal.

Like there was a normal she could get back to. Her normal was gone. She had to create a new normal. That would take time.

And that had to include her following whatever the Lord wanted her to do. That was another thing that Noah seemed to understand and encouraged her in. He didn't preach at her, but his comments were insightful, and they lined up with Scripture. She loved that she had a...friend—that's what he was—who knew the Bible and who she could talk to about spiritual truths.

He would make a great husband.

That was a crazy thought. She just lost a child. She wasn't looking for a relationship, not with anyone. Even if Noah did seem to be rather perfect.

"So she really doesn't need a bottle?"

"Nope. Just like Matt said, horses can drink from a very young age. And Matt just figured he would try the bucket before he tried the bottle, and she drank it. So, that's what we're going to do. That way, she doesn't have to be weaned from the bottle."

"You're saving yourself a step."

"Yeah. Or not doing a step that we don't need to. Since she's drinking just fine from the bucket."

She held the bucket while he opened the stall door.

"I'm assuming we're going to walk in and close it behind us?" he asked.

"Yeah. That's the way Matt did it yesterday, and although she is very tame and not wild at all, I wouldn't want to have to try to chase her around the barn. Although more than that, I wouldn't want her to get hurt on anything."

"You think she'll run into something? Don't horses have very good eyesight?"

"She's still learning to use her legs, but I think sometimes they just get to going too fast and can't quite get stopped in time. Even after they get a little older, you have to watch and be careful. They're like little kids and have tons of energy and love to run."

"There's lots of stuff for them to get hurt on out there then." She assumed he was referring to the tractor that was parked on the barn floor and the various equipment that Matt had around, including a wheelbarrow, a couple rakes and pitchforks and shovels, and that type of thing.

There was plenty for a horse to get into and get hurt on.

"It's a lot easier to prevent an accident than it is to help them get better once they get hurt."

"I'd imagine. That's probably true for pretty much anyone."

"Of course. Of course, there are things that you can't prevent against, and sometimes prevention gets more onerous than it's worth, but you do what you can."

She held the bucket out, and the foal walked forward slowly, cautiously, her ears up, her eyes on them.

"She's adorable," he murmured.

She loved the admiration in his voice, and it made her smile. "Isn't she?"

"Are you thinking of names?"

"Sweetheart."

"Shorten it to Sweetie."

"Something like that." She sighed as the foal nuzzled the edge of the bucket. "I don't know. I guess I just want it to be something special. You know?"

"It's not every day that you get to name a horse."

"This'll be the first horse I've ever named. So yeah. I've gone decades without getting to. I want to make it count."

"Well then, you probably need to take your time and think about it."

"I don't want to think about it too long though, because sometimes when you do that, it ends up getting a name of its own, and then it's impossible to get people to use the name you choose."

"Speaking from experience with...dogs?"

"Cows. I would do this with cows, where it would take me forever to decide on what name I wanted. By the time I decided, the boys had already named it a name that went with its personality. It didn't matter what I said, they only called it their name. We had a Bumper." She lifted her brows at him. "I suppose you can imagine how she got her name."

"Bumping into people?"

"Exactly. Pretty hard actually."

"Any more odd names?" he asked, his eyes on the foal as her nose went into the bucket, and they could hear slurping sounds.

"We had an Eggie. She was born next to a nest of chicken eggs. She ended up breaking them all as she learned to stand."

"And she never shook the name."

"Nope. She was Eggie until she got on the trailer to go to the sale."

"Maybe there's a lesson there about how you have to be careful what you do, because your reputation follows you. And a good reputation is better to build because a bad reputation is hard to shake."

They'd already been serious; she wanted to keep the conversation lighter. "It sounds like you're talking from experience." She slanted a look out of the corner of her eyes and gave him a little grin.

Was she flirting?

He chuckled.

"Come on. What's this reputation that you wish you could shake?"

He laughed outright. "People will call me boring. Although, I guess I'm just as boring now as I was when I was younger. So, I'm not exactly making a big effort to shake it."

"Boring?" She hadn't been expecting that. She thought there was something he had done in his childhood, like wrecking his mother's car or something that had given him a reputation he couldn't get past. "Is that really all the skeletons you have in your closet? You're boring?"

"Don't knock it. Being boring is actually a really big problem. Nobody wants to spend some time with someone who's going to put them to sleep either by talking about stuff that nobody cares about or by thinking about things and missing half the conversation."

"There's nothing wrong with being a deep thinker. There's nothing wrong with talking about things that interest you. You just have to be with the right person who wants to listen."

"Well, for those of us who are boring, maybe finding the right person is difficult."

He was still smiling, but there was a note of seriousness in his tone that made Sunday wonder if he wasn't joking quite as much as he let on.

The foal's mouth came out of the bucket, milk dripping from her lower lip as she looked at them with soft brown eyes.

Her muzzle brushed her arm, like she was looking for more.

"Watch out, she's going to bite you."

"Actually, I don't think they have teeth." She set the bucket down after checking to make sure that it was empty, and then she used both hands to pull the foal's lips up. "Yeah. No teeth."

"Wow. I thought they ate grass. How soon until they come in?"

She laughed. "I don't know. I'm not a horse expert. I just thought I remembered reading somewhere that they're born with no teeth. It's part of the reason we have to be so diligent in feeding her. She can't eat anything yet. If she doesn't have milk, she won't survive."

"That's a heavy responsibility."

"Like being responsible for a baby." She said that before she thought, but it wasn't as awkward as it could have been, because he had a thoughtful look on his face.

"I suppose you're right. Keeping a little human alive would be far more pressure than trying to keep an animal. Although still, having something depend on you for its very life would have to be scary."

He shook his head and laughed a little. "It's crazy that I've never thought about that before."

"You never thought about having children?"

Sunday petted the foal's neck, feeling such a strong kinship with her. The filly had lost her mother, she had lost her child. She wanted to hold her in her arms and never let her go. Comfort her and keep her and make sure she had every advantage she needed to grow up to be a good horse.

She was so silly.

"No. I never did."

"Goodness. I thought about having children when I was still a child myself.

That's the difference between boys and girls, I guess."

"Maybe. I wanted to get the relationship thing down first. I didn't want to have a child with someone who wasn't going to be around to help me raise it. Maybe I was too picky."

His words made her hand freeze. That wasn't a slam; he was just telling her how he had run his life.

"Maybe being a deep thinker is a good thing. After all, if I had thought about that, I wouldn't have chosen Glenn as a father. Look at me now. I have nothing."

"You have a family who loves you. You have a friend who thinks pretty highly of you too. At least one. A whole town of them really. And this foal, who really needs a name, is depending on you too. For today at least."

"Yeah. If I had a house with even a little bit of acreage, I would be asking Matt if I could buy her from him. I don't think he'd charge too much for her, since he saved the mare from the kill pen, and we don't even know what breed it is. Although the mare looked like she might have had some draft in her. Maybe something fancy, like a Friesian or a Gypsy Vanner, with her long mane and tail."

"I didn't even notice the mane and tail."

"Maybe because I grew up with animals. Anyway, I've always loved horses. I knew a lot more about them when I was a kid, though."

"You've probably forgotten more than I ever knew."

They laughed a little together as she stroked one side of the foal's neck and he scratched the other.

"This little gal really loves attention," she murmured.

She had not responded to his comment about the people who loved her. He had called himself a friend who thought very highly of her. She wasn't quite sure exactly what that meant. Maybe nothing. Maybe he was just trying to make her feel better.

"I didn't mean to make you feel bad. That's what I meant. I think about things that nobody else does. Maybe I shouldn't have said boring as much as weird."

"No. Not at all," she said quickly. She didn't want him to think that she thought there was anything wrong with him. Because she didn't. Actually, she admired him. "It's good that you have the foresight to think about those kinds of things. I wish I had."

"I didn't mean to make you sad. I wasn't thinking about that. I was just...explaining why I was boring. I guess I think too much."

"I guess we can argue about this if you want to, but I believe that what you did was smart. Maybe, maybe it held you back a little," she acknowledged. "After all, no one is perfect, and a woman who doesn't look like she would be a good wife and mother today might grow into one."

"There's no guarantee of that."

"Right. There is no guarantee in life at all."

"Maybe I wasn't quite honest."

"What?" she said, her fingers stopping on the smooth, silky fur of the foal as she looked at him. "You lied to me?"

"No. Not like that. I just... I think about things. And it's true that I didn't want to be involved with anyone I didn't think was going to stay with me. But there was a second reason why I'd never thought about having children."

"Okay?" she said, her fingers moving slowly, as she wondered if she really wanted to know this.

His eyes moved back to the foal, and he watched his hand as it lifted from the short mane and settled on the wide forehead, scratching gently. "You know how sometimes you know someone, and they're just so...not perfect. You know they're not perfect. But they're just perfect for you. Or, I don't know. You hold them up as a standard, no one else quite reaches that standard. I kind of had that issue too. I knew everyone I dated wasn't quite what I wanted, because I'd already met the person who was exactly what I wanted. It's kind of hard to lower your standards after that."

She laughed. "I don't have that problem. Glenn was me scraping the bottom of the bucket. The only way I have to go is up, but I don't really want to go at all."

"You don't want to get married again?"

"No. I mean, especially since I lost Blake, I've been lonely. But I don't think being lonely is a good reason to get married. After all, you can be lonely in a marriage. And that's probably a worse loneliness than being lonely and single, because you can't really do anything about it."

"You can go out with friends. It doesn't have to be a romantic relationship."

"That's true. You can surround yourself with friends, jump into the church and get involved, focus on your work and do your very best there, keep yourself busy and active. And to some extent, that's what I've done. That's what I've always done. But there's just the loneliness of living with someone who is supposed to love you but doesn't."

That's as honest as she'd ever been with anyone. It was lonely and hurtful, and hard, because a person was trapped unless they wanted to renege on their marriage vows and find someone else.

"You know, I don't know how this would look, but we're supposed to look to Jesus to fulfill our needs. I don't think we need to be lonely."

"You're probably right. Whether we're married, or whether we're not, Jesus wants to be the One we run to. I am definitely guilty of turning to other things, when I know that Jesus wants me to turn to him."

Sunday appreciated that he had been honest, which made her feel like she could be frank, too. She'd been thinking back over her life. There were so many times where she felt like she was sad and alone, but she really wasn't alone, she didn't have to be alone ever. Jesus was with her. Why couldn't she remember that?

"Sometimes I think the reason He wants us to remember that He is with us is because it gives us hope. After all, when we remember that this world isn't our final destination, that there is more for us, that we have so much to look forward to, we feel hopeful instead of hopeless."

"That's what I'm going to name her." Sunday stroked down the foal's neck and scratched under her throat while she lifted her head up in enjoyment. "Hope."

Chapter 17

"Oh my goodness, I think Ricky pulled a muscle or something."

Noah looked over to see that Sunday's horse was indeed limping quite badly.

"We'd better get off and walk. We can hardly treat him here. He's going to have to make it back to the stable."

"Yeah. I just feel terrible."

"All we were doing was walking. I'm sure it wasn't anything you did."

"No. You're right. I just feel terrible because he's obviously in pain."

Sunday swung out of the saddle, and Noah did as well. He certainly wasn't going to ride his horse while Sunday was walking beside hers.

"I want to check his feet and just make sure that he didn't get something stuck in one. I've never seen a seashell get stuck in a horse's foot, but I suppose it's possible." She reached down, picking up each hoof and checking it thoroughly while he held the reins.

She straightened back up. "Nothing."

"I think these things happen sometimes."

"Yeah. Like a person pulls a muscle putting their shirt on in the morning or something."

"Or sneezing."

"True." They laughed a little, and now that Sunday was off his back, Ricky seemed to be moving a little better.

He checked his watch. "I'm glad we didn't go too far. If we walk back, we should get there with time to spare before it's time to feed Hope again." He loved the name she had given to the horse. He thought that it represented the time she was in in her life right now. Of losing her son, facing the fact that she was alone, but knowing that she had hope.

It made him smile just thinking about it.

"I would feel fine about all of this, except those clouds that have been rolling in are getting darker every minute."

"I couldn't agree with you more on that. The waves are definitely getting bigger as well." They'd been big the whole time they'd been riding, but sometimes that just indicated a storm on the lake that never made it to shore.

Regardless, it looked like this one was coming in.

He tried to judge the distance from where they were to where the stable was.

If they were riding, it would be an easy decision. They would definitely make it. But since they were walking, and not fast, with the horse limping between them, he wasn't sure.

"You want to chance it? Or do you want to stop and take shelter at that abandoned cottage that's just down the beach a bit?"

"I say let's see how we're doing till we get there. What do you think?" she asked, her brow furrowed as she looked at the clouds and then back to him. The whole time, they continued to walk, with Ricky between them, his head bobbing down with each step.

"I guess I wouldn't be too concerned about it, except being caught on the beach in a lightning storm is not safe."

"Exactly." They both knew that, and he was only stating the obvious, which she agreed with immediately.

They walked in silence for a while as the wind kicked up, and the waves continued to roar.

He loved this kind of weather. It always felt invigorating to him. Not to mention, it reminded him of the power of God. Which was very reassuring. If God could control something as powerful as the waves of Lake Michigan, the wind, and the lightning, he could certainly trust God to control his life.

"I think we need to stop. He's not limping any worse, but he's just going slow, and I feel bad pushing him."

"Same. I don't think we're hurting him by making him walk, or I guess I should say I don't think we have a choice."

"I agree. And he's moving everything okay. We know he didn't twist it or break it, so I'm hoping maybe it's just a bruise from perhaps stepping on a seashell or something."

They didn't say anything else, because they could only speculate as to what caused it and what the injury actually was.

A big gust of wind blew droplets of water on them, and Noah lifted his head to it.

"I think you're enjoying this," Sunday accused.

"It's terrible, isn't it? I've always loved storms."

"Don't they scare you?" she asked, sounding incredulous.

"Not really. I mean, I guess in a way they do. And I don't necessarily like that feeling."

"Some people love to be scared. Why else would folks watch horror movies?"

"To laugh?" he suggested, which did elicit a chuckle out of her.

"I never laugh at them. Well, I shouldn't say that. I've only ever watched two. I guess I didn't learn my lesson with the first one, and after the nightmares stopped, after five years, I watched another one. Dumb. Dumb. Dumb."

"I've never even been interested in them. It just seems a little ridiculous. Not to mention, I don't enjoy being scared. And I don't enjoy death and destruction. And I definitely don't enjoy anything that has to do with the spirit world, other than talking to God."

"I'm a little annoyed that you're so smart. Why couldn't I have been intelligent like that?"

"We talked about that some in high school. Back when we were friends." He almost didn't say that last part. He didn't want to rub it in that they used to hang out together.

"You were the best friend I ever had." She didn't seem like she was saying it in order to get a reaction out of him. She couldn't possibly know how that made his heart flip and his chest feel warm and good.

At least she had good memories of him.

"You were a good friend too. I could always count on you to listen to me, even if you didn't always understand."

"I always thought you were interesting. But you're right, I didn't always understand everything you said. Although, I can remember listening to you and wondering where in the world you came up with your ideas. I mean, I never would in a million years think of the things that you thought of."

"I don't know. I just like putting things together in my head, you know, finding patterns and similarities. But I can't really explain it any more than that."

"Well, I think it's neat. And it helps me see things that I normally wouldn't see. Because we definitely don't think the same way."

They had reached a spot where they could cut through the dunes to get to the cottage, so he led his horse first and assumed that Sunday was following behind.

He cut through some of the overgrown weeds, picking his way to make it as easy for Ricky as he could. The sand was a little deeper, and it was harder to walk in.

He stopped for a moment and looked back. "Is Ricky doing okay?"

"This is harder for him, but he's fine. Still slow, but he doesn't seem to be in any great pain."

He didn't say anything more, simply turned around and continued on.

He'd seen the cottage several times while he was walking, but he never stopped to check it out. It might not be much in the way of shelter.

But as they made their way back, he was happy to note that while there were vines growing up the sides and a few boards missing on the steps, the roof looked sturdy.

"We should tie the horses in the back?" he asked as she came up beside him and stopped in front of the porch.

"That would keep them out of the worst of the wind."

She led the way to the back, and he followed.

He thought they were going to have to improvise to find something to tie the horses to, but it turned out that there was a small shed behind the cottage that he hadn't noticed from the beach. It must have been the way the land lay that it sat hidden, but whatever it was, it was just big enough for both horses to fit in.

"Hopefully it doesn't blow over," she said as they closed the door behind them after loosening the girths and taking off the bridles.

"Well, in all the years it's been here, it hasn't blown down yet."

"Today could be the day," she said with more than a little irony in her voice.

"Maybe it's selfish, but I'd rather the shed blow down than the cottage," he said as they walked up the steps, careful to avoid the second step which was missing several boards.

"This would have been a beautiful place to live at one point," she murmured as he carefully opened the door.

"It kind of feels like it might have always been just a summer cottage, never a permanent residence, but I could be wrong."

Normally he would have allowed her to go first, but he didn't know what they might find inside, so he stepped into the cabin himself.

He didn't expect it to be overrun with animals, but a person never knew.

There were no cupboards or counters. All that was in the room was a fireplace and a table with four chairs. One of the chairs lay on its side, like it had been bumped over by something over the years and no one had ever bothered to pick it back up.

The windows were dirty, but they allowed the dim light to filter in, which seemed to be the only light in the cabin.

"There are no switches for electricity." She looked around. "I think you're right.

This was just a little place for people to take a break during the summer."

"It's funny, as close as they lived to Strawberry Sands, I never knew who they were." He pulled a chair out and looked at it. "Do you want me to sit down first to make sure it will hold you?"

"That's sweet. But you don't have to do that."

"I'd rather do that than have you get hurt. We'll have enough trouble getting Ricky back. If I have to carry you and save you like a damsel in distress, that would be terrible."

"It would be even worse if I had to carry you like a knight in distress."

"That doesn't have quite the same ring to it."

"Give me a few minutes, I'll think of something else. Duke in distress?"

"I have no royalty in my bloodlines." His lips pulled back. "At least none that I know of."

"Me either." She seemed a little sad about that.

"Are you sure? Maybe you do. Lots of people have been surprised when they looked into their ancestry and found that they have famous people as great-great-grandparents or something."

"I think it would go further back than great-great, but I suppose it's possible."

"Yeah, I don't know. It's a little overrated. I mean, what does it matter if you have famous people in your ancestry? You don't ride on their laurels. You ride on your own. You make your own life. It doesn't have to be a famous life. Doesn't have to be a life of everyone thinking you're something and you end up missing out on all the important things."

She looked like she thought about that for a little bit. "That's true. I'm thankful for every minute I spent with Blake. I would really regret it if I had lost him, and all I had to look back on were times that I didn't have enough time for him or times I pushed him aside so I could do whatever it was that was making me money or fame or whatever." She laughed, like the idea of her being famous or having a lot of money was silly.

"There were times in my life where I wanted to make more money, be famous, maybe even have a TV show where cameras followed me around and everybody took my business advice to heart, but… That just doesn't seem like a good life. I mean, always being in everyone's eye, having them watch everything you do. On one hand, you have a real platform to help people, but on another hand, you sacrifice so much in order to do it."

"Like time with the people that you love. Giving attention to the people who want it from you. I think that's a better life."

"Yeah, I agree."

"You don't have to say that you agree. Just because of the way you're handling the hotel in Strawberry Sands, I can see that you do. It's obvious that you've wanted to make sure that the community is impacted in a positive way and that you don't take business from, for example, my mom."

"Actually, I want to buy her business. I think there is great potential for growth there."

Her eyes narrowed, and his stomach twisted. He wasn't sure he liked that look.

"It just occurred to me that...you must have a lot of money." She laughed, a soft, derisive laugh. "I know that seems like an obvious thing, but you're just so...unassuming. I was thinking you were just like me, but you're not. You...build hotels for a living. You buy bed-and-breakfasts as investments. You... You're rich."

It didn't sound like it was a compliment. And he didn't know what to say about it. People probably did consider him rich.

"It's not like I have a million dollars in the bank."

"But you do have a million dollars."

He lifted his chin in assent. "In assets, yes. Much more."

"Why did I not see that?"

"Does it change anything?" he asked gently. "Does it make me a different person? Does it change the way you see me? Does it change my character?" He had to ask those questions. Because he felt like it didn't. The money didn't have anything to do with anything. He was the same man, with or without it.

She put an elbow on the table and set her chin in her hand, studying him. "I told you that you think about things I don't. I guess I just automatically assume that you are rich, so we are completely different and couldn't possibly have anything in common. But you're right. You were rich when you helped me feed Hope this morning, and you were rich when you held her mom's head so she could be born. You've been rich when we saddled the horses and went for a ride today. I guess you're right, it doesn't change anything. I just...didn't see it."

"I'm sorry. I should hang a sign around my neck that says 'I'm rich,' that way I won't shock people when they find out." He was only partially joking. After all, sometimes when people found out he was rich, it was almost the same reaction that folks might have when they found out that someone was poor. Or a convict, or a child molester. It just wasn't a good reaction.

"Is there something wrong with being rich?" he asked, knowing what he thought the answer was but also knowing that the answer that Sunday gave was important as well.

"No. There's nothing wrong with it. It's your character that counts. There's nothing wrong with not having money, any more than there is something wrong with having money. It's how you act that matters." She lifted her head and set her hand down on the table.

She smiled a little, and as lightning brightened up the room for just an instant and thunder cracked right behind it, he put his hand down and covered hers with it.

She jumped a little at the sound of the thunder, and he squeezed.

Her hand flipped under his, and before he knew it, their fingers had threaded together.

She was staring at their hands, and he looked down as well, liking the way that looked. Her fingers together with his.

Chapter 18

Dear Business Boy,

I can't believe how much better I feel. I adopted an orphan foal that was born on my brother's farm. At night, he and his family get up and feed her, and I feed her every two to three hours during the day.

I just love that she lost her mother and I lost my son, and God brought us together. I feel like it's a very beautiful thing, and He did it just for me. Oh, and maybe for Hope too.

That's what I named the baby, Hope. Anyway, I appreciate your letters. They've been so helpful to me as I slowly form a new normal. You, and someone that I've been seeing, just as a friend, of course. But he's been there, beside me. You know? When you're lonely, and you don't want someone barging into your life and pushing hard, you just need...a companion. Someone who seems to understand, or if they don't understand, someone who is willing to wait until you show them enough that they do. Anyway, I guess I'm not explaining that very well.

But on a different note, I want to talk to my mom about the idea of selling the bed-and-breakfast. I think that she would like to on the one hand, but on the other, I can see her wondering what in the world she was going to do. I mean, she could be a full-time grandma. She loves that job. But she likes to stay busy as well. I... I feel like she might be a little at loose ends if she didn't have the bed-and-breakfast to keep her busy.

So, you said you were in business. What kind of business do you do? My friend builds hotels apparently. I guess he and I haven't really talked much about him either. It's all about me.

Maybe not all about me. He's interested in Strawberry Sands, because he's moving here.

Sorry. Somehow, I keep going back to that subject. You know how it is when you keep thinking about someone? It's actually gotten to the point where I feel a little guilty because I don't think about Blake nearly like I think I should, and I think about my friend a lot more. I feel like I'm doing Blake a disservice if he's not in my mind constantly. And maybe there's a part of me that's a little afraid that I'll forget about him. I don't want to. I want to always remember him forever and ever.

But at the same time, I want to move on with my life. Is that normal?

Anyway, I see you in a corporate office somewhere, wearing a suit and tie, with your shiny shoes propped up on your desk, as you hold the phone to your ear and work on your laptop at the same time. Is that an accurate picture?

If you want to picture me... I'll warn you this is going to be graphic. I'll be cleaning in my mom's B&B. Probably up to my elbows in the toilet, sweat dripping off my nose, my face beet red because I'm so hot, and I'll look over at my phone and see a text from my mom that says, "They're here! They're two hours early! Is the room done?" And then picture me speed cleaning, using Clorox liberally, and trying to make sure I get everything sanitized.

That's my job.

Except, I do make candy some too. That's my favorite job. That's kind of like my love child. Time in the kitchen, creating things. I haven't done that much since Blake passed, and I didn't do it a whole lot before. It wasn't profitable. Plus, Mom needed help.

But my friend and I were talking about what we wanted to do with our lives and how we wanted them to count. I kind of feel like I can be a bigger blessing to people if I made candy for them. You know, making them smile. Although, I suppose it's a blessing to anyone to have a clean toilet too.

That just doesn't seem quite as romantic. Not to mention, I love making candy, and I hate scrubbing toilets. So there's that.

All right. Please write back, giving more specifics. Give me a picture to think of you as you work. Unless of course my assessment of you with your feet propped up on your desk was accurate?

Your friend,

Lover of the lake

Chapter 19

Dear Lover of the lake,

I laughed at your idea that I sit at my desk with my feet propped up.

At least I was working with one hand. Or maybe two—was that a business call I was on while I held the phone to my ear?

Teasing you just a little.

My days are different. As I'm sure yours are, although I suppose if you're cleaning at a bed-and-breakfast, there's only so much variety you can have.

For me, I might be at the office in Chicago one day, on the field watching a job another day, and I might be taking a trip to France or Germany on another. I have a trip coming up.

I don't really like to travel though. I don't like to be stuck in an airplane for hours on end. Somehow, the crying babies are always seated right beside me. Or behind me. Or in front of me. Actually, I don't really mind the crying babies, but I do mind not being able to move. It's terrible to get a middle seat on a transatlantic flight. Trust me. I've been there.

As for the things I actually do in my business, there's a lot of different things. Maybe that was why I was vague. I can give you all the nitty-gritty, but it would probably bore you. I work a lot in commercial properties. So, I don't build private houses or handle stocks and bonds for individuals. I suppose it's easier to tell you what I don't do than what I do.

But I guess I've always felt that it's more important who a person is than what they do. So many times, we're defined by what we do, we use that as part of our identity, and then, when something changes, or when we're not successful in our business or personal lives, we're devastated.

Did you see yourself as a mother? Not that there's anything wrong with that, but when you lost your son, you lost your identity.

I think that's why it's so important for us to see ourselves as children of God. That should be our identity as someone who is loved by God, who was bought by God with blood. Through death. All those things describe me. I think they probably describe you as well. Maybe that's the more important thing? Do you agree?

I love horseback riding. I haven't done it much, in fact only once, but it was a lot of fun. I think, maybe it's who you're with just as much as the actual riding that makes it fun. I suppose since my experience is limited, I don't know for sure, but the one time I went, I had the best company in the

world. And that made all the difference.

I'd love to go again, but only if I could go with the same person. I don't think I'd want to go with anyone else.

I'm really happy that you're doing better. That's something I've been praying for. I think your mom was wise when she said that time would heal, but I also think that you have to have the right mindset, and you've worked hard to have that. I admire that. Not everyone can do that. And of course, I think people do it at their own pace.

As for worrying about forgetting about your son. I don't think you need to worry about that. A mother doesn't forget her child. Whether that child is with her, or whether he's on the other side of the earth, whether he's in heaven with the Father. But I can understand the fear. You love them, and you don't want them to become obsolete. But they won't. Blake influenced your life. You are the person that you are because of his seven years on this earth.

Isn't that true?

Wouldn't you be a very different person if you hadn't had those seven years with him?

I think that's the thing that's taken me some time to understand. I want the bad people out of my life, but I also owe them a thank you. Because every bad experience I've had, every bad actor I've come in contact with, every dishonest or rotten person who has been in my life, has made me a better person. Whether it's because they opened my eyes to the fact that I might possibly be acting the way they were. Or whether it's because I determined in my heart that I would not be like them, it doesn't matter. They made me better.

Isn't that a paradox? How we should thank the people who have been the worst to us because they've brought out the best in us?

I don't know. Maybe that's not true for everyone. I was just with someone the other day who said of someone they didn't like, "If that's the kind of game they want to play, I can play that game. They want to do that, I'll do that right back to them."

I guess in my heart I was thinking, you're not allowing them to make you better. You're letting them bring you down to their level.

I didn't say that. That person wouldn't have been very receptive. But I guess that's when people who are unkind or mean to us don't make us better. They bring us down.

I don't want to let that happen. Not to me.

I suppose the same thing is true when you lose someone. You say, "Death hurts, and it hurts because I loved them. So I'm never going to love anyone again."

Maybe we say that about marriage relationships too. "I was in a bad one, so I'm never going to be in another one, because I don't want to have that pain again."

Although, as I'm writing that, there's a certain amount of wisdom there. After all, I'm terrible at picking people to be in relationships with. It just makes sense that I probably shouldn't do it again. I don't know. I think about weird things sometimes.

Thanks for your letter. It made me smile.

Your friend,
Business Boy

Chapter 20

Dear Business Boy,
Maybe you should try sitting at your desk with your feet propped up on it. Perhaps that would be more comfortable. Definitely more comfortable than sitting in the middle seat on a transatlantic flight with a baby crying beside you or behind you or in front of you, or wherever. I can't hear a baby crying without wanting to go over and try to help. But sometimes, they just

need to cry. Especially on airplanes. Earbuds make that a lot easier now, I think.

Anyway, I'm just trying to help. You know, stretch your horizons a little. I'm saying that sarcastically, since you've traveled the world, and I haven't gone anywhere. I've always lived here. I haven't even seen the ocean, let alone flown over top of it. I think I just prefer to be beside Lake Michigan. I've never felt like I was missing anything by not seeing the ocean.

Is it a lot different than the lake?

Hope is growing. I can almost see her getting bigger every day. Her teeth are coming in, and we started her on some milk replacer pellets. I can give her her bucket of milk and then put a little milk in with the milk replacer pellets. She's got teeth and can chew a little, but the milk makes them softer so she can just lap it up if she wants to.

She eats a lot.

It makes me happy to watch her. It's kind of funny how an animal can't talk, can't really relate to you at all, and yet you can feel such an affinity for them that they feel like a friend.

She's just a baby, and yet I consider her a friend.

Maybe that's why God made animals, to help us through the hard times in our lives. When people just don't have the patience to listen over and over again to the things that I need to run through my mind before I can finally accept them.

You are one of two exceptions to that. But I don't know, maybe you just skim through my letters and don't actually read what I write. But I appreciate you being a person I can write to, because writing is kind of therapeutic. And whether you read it or not, it's helped me to get it out on paper.

Where are you going on your trip? When? We're hitting the busy season of summer, and the bed-and-breakfast is full almost every single day. I haven't gotten the courage up to ask my mom yet, but I suppose I should. My friend hasn't said anything more about it, but I know he was serious. Whenever he's in town, he comes with me to feed Hope. I think he likes her as much as I do. And I enjoy spending time with him. Probably more than I should.

Thanks for letting me write to you.

Your friend,

Lover of the lake

Chapter 21

Dear Lover of the lake,

I agree with you about animals. I think dogs make the best friends, maybe because they seem to love us no matter what we do. And most dogs are in a perpetual good mood. Although I had a dog growing up who was a real grump. She was a small mixed breed, and every once in a while, she would get the urge to play, but most of the time, she wanted to sit around and be left alone. Still, she was a great companion, and I enjoyed spending time with her throughout my childhood. There aren't too many memories outside of school where she wasn't with me.

I'm sure horses are different in a lot of different ways, but I kind of understand. If I had a bad day at school, or if I got a bad grade on a test, my parents might be upset with me, but my dog just licked my hand and loved me anyway.

I guess maybe a dog's love might be the closest to the kind of love that God has for us. I know there's no comparison, but whatever we do, God loves us anyway, just like a dog. Isn't that true?

I think I remember hearing a poem somewhere that talked about a dog's love being similar to God's love. Maybe that's where I got the idea. Or maybe it's just because I lived it, and I've experienced it. That's the best way to learn, isn't it?

I don't know what to say about your mom. I think there is a risk that she'll feel unneeded. You know? If your friend offers to buy the bed-and-breakfast from her, he might make her feel that she isn't needed around Strawberry Sands, and from what I understand, your mom's a real blessing everywhere she goes. You wouldn't want her to feel bad.

At the same time, having all that stress and strain and, most of all, all of that work taken off her hands might be a true blessing. I think you have a good enough relationship with your mom and you could just ask her, don't you?

It's nice to hear the updates about Hope. And it's good that your friend goes with you. I'm guessing that he wouldn't do it if he didn't enjoy it.

Either that, or he enjoys spending time with you. Maybe both. It sounds to me like you really like each other and get along well. Sometimes when you're with someone who isn't like you, they complement you. Have you noticed that?

When I'm doing business, I often try to find people who are different than I am, who have strengths in areas where I don't, to work with. I think so often we look for people who are the same. And it's true, we tend to get along better with people we understand and who do things exactly the way we do. But in my experience, I am a stronger and better person if I'm with someone who has strengths where I have weaknesses, and we somehow manage to still get along. I think learning to get along with people is one of the hardest things to do in life. Especially people who aren't like us. Sometimes I wonder if that's not why God made opposites attract. Because He knows that people we don't agree with, people who irritate us, people who have different personalities and skills than we do help shave the rough edges off us and help us become better people.

Maybe that's just me making things up, but it seems to me that God did that for a reason.

Too many times, you want to throw in the towel and give up on people, move on to someone who gets us or whatever. And we never take the time to consider ourselves and that we might become better if we change and grow, using the principles of the Bible.

That's as close to marriage therapy as I'll ever get. And coming from someone who's never been married, maybe you should just ignore it.

It used to be that people would ask me when I was getting married, but I think everyone's given up on that. Maybe you'll get that. I never knew what to say. Did they want me to get married just for the sake of getting married? Or did they want me to wait until God brought the right person into my life?

Sometimes God brings the right person into your life, but it's not the right time, or maybe He brings them in, knowing it's not the right time, because He wants you to forge a friendship with them first.

I would only say that if you're not married. It's not a good idea to have good friends of the opposite sex if you're married. I've seen so many people end up in cheating situations with people that they were "just friends" with.

I told you that was all the marriage counseling advice I had, but I guess I had a little more.

I'm going to drop that subject.

I'm going to Mexico. A resort in Cancún. I know, it's a rough life.

Anyway, it's a business trip, and while the scenery will be nice, and I'll enjoy it, it's not like I'm going there for relaxation or with people I love.

I really enjoy writing to you. I know that you are the one going through a hard time, but it's been a blessing to me as well.

Thank you.

Your friend,

Business Boy

Chapter 22

"Can you tell me who has box number forty-three?" Sunday asked Mrs. Miller as she stood on the other side of the counter of the post office in Strawberry Sands.

Mrs. Miller, her gray hair curled close to her head, her glasses perched on the end of her nose, a golden chain that led from one side arm to the other dripping down to her shoulders on both sides, peered across the counter at Sunday.

"This is a government institution. I cannot divulge that information." Her face was serious, but then she broke into a smile, her eyes twinkling. "But if you want to know who's pregnant, you can go ahead and ask. Because I know that news, and I can tell you."

"Who's pregnant?" Sunday asked, swallowing her disappointment that she couldn't find out who owned PO Box forty-three.

She'd been thinking about coming to the post office for a while, trying to figure out who Business Boy was. She was curious, she had to admit. She wanted to meet him, but she wanted to know who she'd been talking to all this time first. It had to be someone who lived in Strawberry Sands, as he answered her letters so frequently. He'd said he had a business but didn't want to divulge the details. Did that mean it wasn't legit? That he didn't really have a business? That he was just trying to hide it?

She was suspicious.

"Your sister, Clara Landry." Mrs. Miller's voice trembled with excitement. "Well, she is Clara Hudson now." She rubbed her hands together. "I just heard this morning, directly from her. She said she was keeping the news to herself for a little bit, but if she told me, you know she didn't mean that."

Sunday's brows went up. Her sister was pregnant? She hadn't heard a word.

Maybe Clara was just so excited that she couldn't contain herself. Probably she was going to announce it to the family on Sunday at their regular Sunday dinner. Usually Sundays were her mom's busiest check-out day, but they often tried to have dinner together as a family at the bed-and-breakfast if they could.

This time of year, they often ended up going outside and eating around the campfire. Sometimes the guests joined them, and everyone had a good time.

It wasn't the best place to tell everyone news a person wanted to keep secret, but it would work.

Now Sunday wanted to seek her sister out and congratulate her. She was going to be an aunt again. That was exciting.

And all of her was happy. Although there was a part of her that was a little bit sad. It didn't take away from her excitement about her sister, it just reminded her that she had had a baby once. And now he was gone.

She supposed that was something she needed to get used to since it would probably be something she would think about for the rest of her life.

"I'll have to find her and congratulate her. That's so exciting."

Mrs. Miller nodded her head. "It's so thrilling to see you girls who grew up here in town staying here and having babies. So many people move away. It can be hard. This was definitely a ray of sunshine, and I can't wait to tell every-one I see."

Sunday nodded, and she tried to look a little pathetic, to play on Mrs. Miller's sympathies. After all, she just heard that her sister was having a baby, and she had lost her son not that long ago. Surely the woman could feel a little bit bad for her and maybe tell her something that she didn't usually tell customers.

"Are you sure you can't tell me who owns box forty-three?"

"Well, I can't tell you who it is. But I can tell you that their permanent address is in Chicago."

That didn't really help. Except, Business Boy had said he had an office in Chicago. Of course, the address might not be an office. It might be an apartment building or something he made up.

"Thanks, Mrs. Miller," Sunday said, trying not to sound as dejected as she felt as she pushed the door open and walked outside.

Was there some other way she could learn the identity of Business Boy? She couldn't think of anything, and it was time for her to go feed Hope again.

She smiled at the thought. Nodding at the strangers on the street, tourists most likely, she walked down to the bed-and-breakfast.

Her mom was sitting on the porch with Clara, and after checking the time and seeing that she had a few minutes to spare, Sunday did a ninety-degree turn and walked in the gate to the bed-and-breakfast.

"Sunday! I have news. And I'm sorry, I haven't been able to not tell anyone, although I wanted to tell my family first!"

"Let me guess, you got a dog?" Sunday said, knowing what the news was but teasing her a bit.

"No! Almost, you're very close."

"Hmm, very close to buying a dog. Let's see, you sold a painting for six figures?" Her sister was a painter, and since she got married, her husband, Alex, had been encouraging her to give her art the time it deserved.

"No, although that would be awesome." Her sister practically glowed. "You give up?"

"You bought a boat?"

"You're never going to guess. Actually, I thought you would." Then her eyes narrowed. "Where were you?"

Sunday smiled. "The post office?"

"You know! You little turkey." She laughed, running across the porch and wrapping her sister in a hug.

"I do know. Congratulations. I'm so excited for you."

Her sister squeezed her extra hard and then pulled back a little. "Are you? I was afraid it would make you sad."

"I'm fine. You guys don't have to treat me with kid gloves anymore. I promise, I'm fine. And I really am happy for you. You and Alex are going to be the best parents ever."

She meant those words with all her heart, truly she did.

"When are you due?" she asked, wrapping her arm around her sister's waist and walking up the steps to the porch.

"At the end of February. We're going to find out whether it's a boy or girl, and we're going to tell everyone the name when we figure out what it's going to be. Which we haven't yet."

"I take it you've been asked those questions a hundred times today." There was humor in her voice. She remembered what it was like to be pregnant.

"Exactly."

"You look like you're feeling just fine. No morning sickness?"

"A little. But usually just in the evening. Which makes me feel like it was not well named."

"No. It can be anytime sickness. But I suppose if you're sick in the evening, it doesn't really say as much to you as it might if you were not well in the morning."

"That's so true. It never occurred to me that it was related to pregnancy until my midwife told me it probably was. I was worried because I lost a little weight."

"I think it's normal to do that in the first trimester."

"That's what the midwife said." She snorted. "I could skip the midwife visit and just go to you."

"I'm glad you went to her. She probably gave you a prescription for prenatals, which I cannot do."

"That's true." They sat down in white rocking chairs, one on either side of their mom.

Sunday noticed that their mom glowed. She loved being a grandma, loved having the kids so close, and loved being able to spend time with them. This was probably the best news she'd heard in a while.

They talked about the baby for a while and about the school that Clara and Alex had bought and renovated. They'd moved in, and Alex was running his business from home while Clara painted and helped him.

Sunday couldn't help but be a little bit jealous. They were so happy. And Alex was a good man. Clara had made a wise decision, unlike Sunday.

The jealousy wasn't wishing that Clara didn't have what she had. It was just wishing that Sunday had been smarter, or more patient, or something.

But she supposed that kind of jealousy was just as bad as any other kind, so she tried to shove those thoughts aside and just realize that God could still make her life beautiful, even if it was in the way He chose, instead of the way she did.

After they'd talked for a while, they rocked silently for a couple of minutes, and Sunday decided she could reach out tentatively to her mom.

"Have you ever thought of selling the bed-and-breakfast?"

Her mom stopped rocking and jerked her head back, although she didn't look upset, just surprised.

"I suppose over the years there have been times where I wish I wasn't busy all the time. Where I wish I could go places when I wanted to instead of trying to schedule them around when guests were scheduled to arrive. Sometimes I'd like to sleep in. But I suppose it's good for me to have to get out of bed. Otherwise, I end up lying around all day. I wouldn't get my day started until dinnertime."

Sunday laughed. She couldn't imagine her mom lying around in bed until dinnertime. Not that there was anything wrong with that exactly. Some people just had a later internal clock than others. But not her mom.

"What if someone came to you today with an offer?" She thought of Noah. He mentioned the bed-and-breakfast once more, and she said she hadn't had a chance to talk to her mom about it. He didn't seem like he was in a huge hurry or that he would even be that upset if she didn't want to.

But if she did, she thought he was ready to make an offer almost immediately.

"I suppose it depends on how good the offer is. I don't even know what the place is worth."

"Alex said property values are going up because of Blueberry Beach and how commercialized that's becoming. It's spreading north, and he thinks we're next."

"I hate to see us get commercialized, although I suppose it's inevitable with a hotel going in. That's worried me some. I've wondered if it would run me out of business. Might be smarter to sell before that happens."

"Or maybe you'll get busier."

"That's what Alex says will happen. He thinks the horses will be a big draw, especially since Chi and Griff and Rodney have their Percheron team. They could run those poor horses all day long every day. Since they only give rides at sunrise and sunset, Chi just told me that they're booked clear through the end of September. Every single day."

"You're kidding!" Lena said, like she couldn't believe it. But then, her look became thoughtful. "I guess I have noticed that our reservations stretch into September as well. I think I have almost every room in the bed-and-breakfast booked every weekend through then. I need to check the books to be sure, but... I know July and August are booked solid."

"So maybe that's right. Maybe Strawberry Sands is going to grow just like Blueberry Beach did, although maybe not in the same way. It's a little more..."

"Rural. Because of the pasture and the horses, it's just not quite as classy, for lack of a better word, as Blueberry Beach."

"I can see that. And I think that's true. So Alex really does think it's going to grow?" It was interesting that Alex and Noah had the same thoughts.

"He does. He thinks Noah is extremely smart for building a hotel. He also thinks that the hotel will actually help business at the bed-and-breakfast." Clara looked at her mom. "I would make sure that you don't sell it for too little, and I do think you could get a good bit out of it." She named the price they'd heard that Chi and Griff had paid for their house on the bluffs. It was quite a lot of money.

"I think you could get that much or even more. This is a turnkey business, and you make a profit every year. Plus, this setting is idyllic, and you have customers who come back year after year, which are all selling points. I think your house is just as many square feet as theirs, although I could be wrong about that."

"That's something I'll have to think about," Lena said, and she seemed un-affected. It seemed like all of Sunday's fears that she might feel pushed out were unfounded. "What do you think about it? Would you mind if I sold out?"

"I'm okay with it. I don't want to see you leave Strawberry Sands though. You could move in with us. There's plenty of room in the schoolhouse." Clara actually looked excited about the idea of her mom moving in. "You could help me with the baby!"

Lena smiled. "That's tempting. I don't think I would mind that at all. But I might miss the interactions with the guests." She looked at Sunday. "What do you think?"

"Maybe you want to ask all the other kids, but I'm fine with it. There is the little house that Clara used to stay in. We could add on to it so that there is a washer and dryer and everything you need in it, and you could just make a condition of the sale that you get to stay in that for as long as you want to."

"That's a good idea," Lena said, nodding as she considered it. "But you're right. I'll probably have to run it past the rest of the kids. I don't want to do something that's going to upset everyone."

"I think you need to do what's best for you, Mom. No one is going to get upset if you make decisions that benefit yourself. You've spent your whole life thinking about others."

"And I'll spend the rest of my life doing the same. Just because you get old doesn't mean all the sudden you get to start thinking about yourself all the time and not being concerned about others. That's not the way this works."

Sunday closed her mouth. Her mom was absolutely right. But how many times had she heard that? That someone had thought about others long enough, and it was time for them to take care of themselves. She couldn't find that in the Bible. The only thing that came even close was Jesus going out to pray. But that wasn't Jesus doing self-care, that was Jesus communing with his Father. It was obvious to her that there was a big difference between making decisions that benefited oneself and taking time to have a relationship with God.

The conversation moved on to other topics, and Sunday enjoyed chatting with her mom until she excused herself to go feed her foal. She was excited, not just to see Hope, but because Noah had been meeting her there most feedings. She had to admit, she was looking forward to seeing him again.

Chapter 23

"You want to buy that orphan foal? Why? She's not worth anything." Matt looked at Noah like he was crazy.

He could hardly admit to the man that he was in love with his sister and wanted to buy the horse so that he could give it to her.

"Sunday said that she thought there was some draft in the mother and perhaps a little bit of a fancy breed."

"Sunday was horse crazy when she was a kid. She probably knows every breed known to man and could give us an in-depth rundown on each of them." Matt rolled his eyes and leaned on the pitchfork he held in his hand.

Noah had come to talk to Matt, but when he'd seen he was working, he'd grabbed a pitchfork and given him a hand.

Now that they had hay in every stall, he also leaned on his and faced Matt. He didn't think Matt was going to tell him no, but he was afraid he was going to try to pry a reason out of him, and he didn't want that.

He didn't need Sunday's brother knowing that he had a crush on his sister.

Especially since he wasn't sure how Sunday felt about him.

Was it terrible that he still wanted to do something nice for her?

This wasn't exactly something a friend did for another friend, but maybe friends who helped deliver a foal together were a little different than friends who hadn't. He never had a friend like that, so he wouldn't know.

"I don't even know where to begin to think about what to charge for her. I suppose if I tried to give her to you, you'd argue with me." Matt's callused hand gripped the top of his pitchfork while he looked at Noah.

"I think I should pay for her. You got some fees in her, notably the milk replacer, which I understand isn't cheap, along with the pellets. Plus, those middle-of-the-night feedings aren't easy."

"What are you going to do with her?"

That was the question he hadn't wanted to answer. But he held Matt's eyes as he answered, "I'm going to give her to your sister."

"Sunday?" Matt asked, surprised, then calculation entering his eyes. "I always suspected in school that you had a huge crush on her."

"I did."

There was no point denying it. As much as he might want to. It was the truth. They were friends, and he liked her as a friend, but he always wanted to be more. There wasn't anything wrong with having a romantic relationship with someone whom he was friends with. As long as it didn't end badly. That could mess up a great relationship.

He assumed that if he and Sunday got together, they'd make sure things worked out. He wasn't the kind of person to go into a relationship and not put everything he had into making it work.

He wouldn't be attracted to Sunday if he thought she was that kind of person either.

"Now you're back, and you still have a crush on her."

He stared at Matt. Was it a crush? A crush made it sound like he was still in high school and had an infatuation with the pretty girl. Sunday was a lot more to him than just a pretty girl.

"I wouldn't call it a crush."

"What would you term it?" Matt asked, like he had the right to or something.

Noah almost told him to shove it, but Sunday was his sister, and she didn't have a dad. He did appreciate her brother protecting her, if that's what this was.

"I guess I have serious intentions toward her, if she'll have me. I haven't figured out whether she will or not, and she hasn't said. But I know she loves the horse, I know she's been a help to her since she lost her son. She's really attached to her, and I wanted to make sure that she doesn't have to worry about you selling her, not that I thought you would.

But if she gets her, there might be a way she can keep her up in the stable next to her mom's house where she's been staying."

"I thought she was gonna try to move back to her apartment."

"She might. But if the horse is there, she might stay at least until she doesn't need to supplement her so frequently anymore." He wasn't sure what she might do, but he wanted her to have the options. He wanted her to be able to make the choices. She'd had a lot of choices made for her, and while he knew that God was in control and allowed those things to happen to her, he wanted her to have the control over this if she could.

Plus, the horse really did mean a lot to her.

"I see. That might be a good thing. I know I'm getting tired of getting up in the middle of the night, and my girls, instead of arguing about who gets to feed her, are arguing about who has to. It would actually take a lot of weight off my shoulders." He narrowed his eyes. "Are you sure Sunday wants her?"

"I figured I'd check with you before I checked with her. I didn't want her to get excited before I knew for sure that you didn't already have plans for her."

"No. I don't have any plans. Other than to try to keep her from dying. That was my only goal."

They shared a look, with Noah figuring he knew what Matt meant. Things had been touch and go for a while, and there was no guarantee that an orphan foal would live. It had been enough of a blow to lose the mom.

He thought that Matt might understand what he was doing. He probably had sympathy for him too, if he thought he was good enough for his sister.

Noah considered just outright asking.

He wasn't sure he wanted to hear the answer.

"Is this okay with you?" he finally asked, figuring that that was a little less difficult to say than "Am I good enough for your sister?"

"Yeah. I kinda thought back in high school you two would get together, and I wish you would have. Glenn was a stupid detour that caused her more hurt than anything."

"I think she's better because of it."

"I guess we all probably are. But it's never easy to watch someone you love go through something hard like that. Glenn had a really great wife, and he treated her terribly. He had an amazing son, and he barely even noticed him. I really wanted to grab a hold of the guy."

But of course he wouldn't. And Noah understood that wasn't a threat, it was just Matt making a statement. Talking about Sunday and letting Noah know how much he thought of her and what he wanted for her.

"Hey, guys. You look so serious." Sunday walked into the barn. She smiled at Noah, and he nodded at her, then she turned her attention to Matt. "You're slow today. Usually, you're out of here by now."

"I've not been scheduling rides during the hottest part of the day. Just to give the horses a break, although I have people clamoring for them. I've been thinking about getting more, but we need more ground."

"That's a problem. It's kind of limited around here. There's this big pile of water that takes up a lot of space." She laughed, and Noah thought about how far she'd come since almost two months ago when she'd been standing at the casket at her son's funeral.

He admired her more today than he had then, and he felt like he knew her better too.

He couldn't help but wonder what she thought of him.

"I was wondering if you wanted to go to the diner and grab a bite to eat after we feed Hope? I had to walk down by it, and Griff is making his onion soup bread again, and it smells delicious. Plus, they had a brochure on the door that said there were strawberry banana smoothies along with strawberry lemonade cake." She lifted her brows. "I hope Hope knows how much I love her that

I walked by the diner and came down here to feed her."

"I don't think there's any doubt in anyone's mind how much you love Hope," Noah said.

Matt smirked, but he didn't say anything. Noah wondered if he might spoil the surprise, but he didn't.

Matt finished up and left while they fed Hope and rubbed her down.

"I've been reading that it's important that orphan foals are with another horse so they learn how to be a horse."

"Interesting. I guess it makes sense that their mother teaches them that."

"Yes. And horses are very social animals. They're herd animals. They need to have other horses around them."

"I see." Maybe his idea of buying Hope had been a bad one. Or maybe there would be another orphan foal that they could get to grow up with Hope, so she'd have a companion.

"Does it have to be an older horse? Or can it be one their own age?"

"I think it can be any horse, but it said if you let it get too attached to you, then it starts to think that you are its mom, and they can get a little rowdy and out of control. Especially as it gets bigger." She looked at Hope, who had been growing almost visibly before their eyes. "Because she has a little bit of draft horse in her, we have to be careful, because she's going to be a big girl."

"I see." Maybe he could ask Matt if he had any suggestions of where he could find another orphan foal. He had a feeling that Sunday would be in her element raising two. But he would talk to Sunday before he did that. She might not want the responsibility. Although, he would make sure she understood that he would stand behind any expenses incurred.

Forty-five minutes later, they were walking back up the sidewalk toward the diner.

"Maybe there will be some seats open now. When I walked by before, there were people standing waiting to be seated."

"I'm glad it's been thriving. And it's important that they're busy this time of year."

"I'm happy for them too."

They walked side by side, as they had more than once over the last few weeks, although he hadn't attempted to hold her hand again. Not since waiting out the storm in the cottage.

She had said something at one point about needing time to get over her son, and he didn't want to push her for more than what she was ready to give.

But when their hands brushed, and then her fingers reached out and touched his, he didn't resist.

Instead, he smiled and allowed her to take his fingers.

He wasn't sure exactly what that meant, to her anyway. For him, it made his heart happy. He didn't go around holding hands with just anyone.

Maybe this was a good time to ask her. He no sooner thought that than the words came out of his mouth. "I just talked to your brother about buying Hope."

"You did?" She seemed shocked. Like she hadn't considered that. "But... You're building a hotel. You...don't even have a house. You're living above the old diner in an apartment. What are you going to do with a horse?"

He let her talk, ask her questions, and waited for her to fall silent again.

"Give her to you."

That really made her jaw drop, and she stumbled a little.

His hand squeezed hers, and he tried to steady her as she started walking again. Slower. Like she couldn't walk and think about this much and process something so difficult at the same time.

"For me?"

"I felt like you were made for each other. If you don't want her, nothing is set in stone. But if you do, Matt's willing."

"But… I'm not any better set up to take care of a horse than you are. Plus, she needs a companion."

"I was thinking we could get another one. Surely there's another orphan foal around who needs someone to take care of it. But if that's too much for you—"

"No! I would love it. This has been… It's been really awesome." She let out a breath and looked at the ground. "It was exactly what I needed. Just… Everything has been exactly what I needed. You, of course, and…" Her voice trailed off, like she was going to say something and then didn't. He wondered if she was going to mention the letters that she'd been writing to Business Boy.

He didn't ask. He didn't want that uncomfortable association. He needed to figure out a way to admit that was him.

"Yeah. If we can figure something out—"

"I kind of thought if your mom is willing to sell the bed-and-breakfast, we could house her there in the barn. Even if she's not, she might be willing to let you keep her there. I would take care of all the expenses, you would take care of the horses themselves, and she wouldn't have to do anything. But I wouldn't want to impose. It's just... That's where you've been staying."

"I've been thinking about moving back to the candy shop. And I think I can, even if we do this, once the baby doesn't need to be fed at night anymore. I can get up in the morning, walk up to the bed-and-breakfast, and feed her. That's not hard at all. It's such a short walk; it would be good for me every morning and every evening."

"Even in the cold and snow of a Michigan winter?"

"Even then."

They had reached the diner, and Noah put a hand on the door, opening it for Sunday. He didn't want to let go of her hand. Maybe she was feeling the same way, because she walked in without letting go of his.

He grinned to himself. He liked this. Liked what it said to him, liked what it said to the town. He hoped he wasn't misjudging.

"Hey!" Chi, the co-owner of the diner with her husband, Griff, hurried toward the door. She looked hassled, with her hair up in a sloppy bun, four pens sticking out of it, and her apron food stained from the day's work.

Still, she was grinning from ear to ear.

"Rodney wanted me to say something to you. I saw you go by earlier, but I was taking an order and I couldn't stop to catch you. I've been watching for you to walk back up ever since. I assumed you were feeding the foal?"

Chi finished speaking as she finally stopped in front of them, giving Sunday a quick hug.

Which Sunday returned.

Chi greeted Noah, and then she turned back to Sunday.

"Rodney wanted you guys to know that he'd been keeping a slot open for you because he'd heard that you guys wanted to take a ride on his Percherons." She looked around the diner and then lowered her voice. "I cannot believe how popular this has been. That sand buggy, with those wide wheels, that Cord Stryker designed for us, is a dream. And those horses are amazing on the beach. People come down just to take pictures of whoever he's driving around. Total strangers. It's crazy."

"It's beautiful. I sat and watched it several times myself and took a picture or two of total strangers myself," Sunday said with a little smile.

"I'm so happy to see you smiling. We were concerned about you. What a hard thing."

Sunday nodded. "It was a hard thing, and I'm not quite ready to say that it was a good thing, but I think someday I will be able to say that." She gave a look of peace to Chi, who gave her another hug.

"All right. Four o'clock is the time he said. I hope you guys can make it."

"I'd love to do it." Sunday looked at Noah.

"Me too. It was awfully nice of him to make time in his schedule. I'm sur-prised."

"You guys have been around together a good bit, and I think he fancies himself a matchmaker. Don't tell him I told you." Chi gave them a knowing look, and then she waved around the diner. "Sit any place there is room. I'll be right over to take your orders." She started to turn and then stopped. "You can probably smell the onion soup bread. It is divine. People are raving about it, especially because Griff has developed a cheesy butter to go with it. It is amazing. Plus, you probably saw our specials on the door, strawberry lemonade cake and strawberry banana smoothies. They have been going like crazy too."

She waved a hand as she turned and hurried away.

"I am dying of starvation. Her talking about the onion soup bread and the cheesy butter? That sounds like a meal in itself."

"To you and me both. I wonder how big a loaf is?" Noah said as he indicated for her to lead the way to whatever seat she wanted.

"I don't know, but if they sell it by the loaf, that's probably the way to go. I think between the two of us, we could eat a whole one ourselves."

"I think she says I eat a lot," Noah said as he slid into the opposite side of the booth. Still holding her hand, their clasped fingers resting on top of the table between them.

He wanted to ask what it meant. She had been the one to take his hand. She had been the one to hold tight when she walked in. But maybe it was better to just let it go. To not probe too deeply. After all, he just said he wanted to buy Hope for her, and surely she knew that meant he cared for her.

Not that gifts showed affection, but it was less about the gift and more about something that soothed her heart and soul after the loss of her son. It was about him wanting her to smile.

They kept their conversation light the whole way through their meal, which consisted of an entire loaf, fresh out of the oven, of onion soup bread along with the special cheese butter that Griff had come up with to go on it. It was soft and warm and oozing butter, and perfect.

They topped it off with a strawberry banana smoothie and decided that they might come back for a piece of strawberry lemonade cake later.

They left the diner, and Noah was so full he felt like he could roll down the sidewalk.

Somewhere during their meal, he lost her hand, and he wasn't sure how she felt about him taking it back.

"That's nice that Rodney kept a time for us. Have we been in the diner that much?"

"Maybe he sees us going down the sidewalk to feed Hope. I just think it's sweet that he fancies himself a matchmaker."

She thought it was sweet. He wondered what she actually thought of them being a couple.

Regardless, he decided he wasn't going to worry about it, that they'd just enjoy the beautiful Michigan summer day, the light breeze, and the relaxing ride with the beautiful Percherons along the lakeshore.

He couldn't think of too many things that he'd rather be doing. Especially since he had to leave on his trip and wouldn't be back for a couple of weeks. Maybe he was hoping for too much, because Sunday seemed sad about it when he told her he had to be away for a while, but he thought she had as good of a time as he did.

He could have a million more days like the one they shared and he wouldn't tire of them. Not ever.

Chapter 24

Lena walked down the sidewalk, smiling as she saw the Percherons riding along the lake. Her hands went to her heart when she saw that it was her daughter Sunday sitting in the carriage along with Noah.

What a romantic ride. The horses were beautiful, with their manes and tails flowing in the breeze, and it looked like Sunday and Noah were deep in conversation as each of them threw back their heads and laughed.

As she watched, Lena realized that perhaps Sunday had asked her about selling the bed-and-breakfast because Noah was interested in buying it. That would make a lot of sense to her, since he was the one building the hotel, and he seemed to think that there were busi- ness opportunities in Strawberry Sands.

It would make her heart so happy if Noah and Sunday got together, and they took over running the bed-and-break- fast. That made her whole soul smile.

But the issue that she'd been having was still there.

What would she do?

Her children looked at her and saw an old lady, but she was just fifty-five. She didn't feel like an old lady. She didn't feel as old as the lady who looked back at her every morning in the mirror. When had she gotten gray hair? When had she gotten those wrinkles around her eyes and mouth? When had her cheeks started to sag? When had she put on these extra pounds that took away her hourglass figure and gave her a matronly look?

She looked like a grandmother.

She knew she had grandchildren, and she loved them, but she didn't feel like a grandmother. She felt like a young girl. A teenager. Maybe someone in her twenties. Certainly not someone who was looking at the late middle of their life. Knowing that her life was already half over. When had that happened? And what was she going to do with the rest of it? Especially if she sold the bed-and-breakfast. It was all she knew.

Enjoying the look of the horses as they trotted along the beach, seeing the others in the field, and the great deep blue of Lake Michigan and a hot summer day just beyond, grounded her a little bit.

It wasn't like she wasn't doing any good for anyone. She set out at a brisk pace, heading north on the lakeshore toward the lighthouse and her friend.

The bed-and-breakfast had been too busy for her to take any time away in the morning. She'd been having to wait until afternoon, when most of the guests had checked out and she had most of the rooms cleaned.

Today, she had a lot of guests staying over, so she didn't have quite as much cleaning to do, and she felt like she could splurge and take a walk to the lighthouse.

Sunday would be back soon and see the note that she left on the counter.

And that was the other thing, Sunday really wanted to make candy again, but she probably would never be comfortable in her candy shop or the apartment that she shared with Blake.

It would be good for her to completely change her location. The bed-and-breakfast would be just the place.

Lena knew they weren't pushing her aside, but it felt a little that way. Like she was old, too old to be good for anything other than spoiling grandchildren and sitting on a rocking chair.

She had lots more life left in her.

She knew if she truly didn't want to sell, her kids wouldn't want her to. She also knew, if she wanted to sell, all of her kids would be fine with it. She didn't think any of them would want to buy, except perhaps Ryan, who had settled back in but still seemed a little restless.

She wouldn't be surprised if he went back out on the rodeo circuit.

Her thoughts went to Ryan, and her mother's heart tried to think of something she could do that would ground him a little better.

She suspected that he was running from something, but she had no idea what. She wouldn't pry into his affairs, although she would certainly never turn away if he wanted to talk to her. She could only pray that he would or go to someone for godly counsel.

Before she knew it, the lighthouse had come into view, with Joe Pianse sitting out the way he usually did in a chair, his fishing pole stuck in the sand, his hat pulled down low over his head.

She smiled when she saw he had two chairs set up.

He'd taken to doing that last summer, grudgingly telling her that she might as well sit down while she stood around and bugged him.

She knew he didn't really think that she was a bother, and he enjoyed the company.

She walked over and sat down.

"Business is slow, isn't it?" he said in his gruff voice.

"Actually, it's busier than ever. How's the fishing?"

"Terrible. Terrible." That's what he always said. "But I do have a few you can take home and fry up for the kids tonight if you want to."

"Maybe we'll make them over a campfire. Are you sure you don't want to come down and join us?" She always invited him, and he always declined. It was a ritual they went through.

"Nah. I'm too busy up here. But the kid was here over the weekend, and he left more espresso beans for you."

She smiled.

"I know that's the only reason you come up here anymore."

It was no such thing, but she had to admit that she was definitely addicted to espresso beans. And it was all Joe's son's fault. She'd never met the man, and from what Joe said, he didn't spend nearly enough time with his father, but Joe complained about everything, and Lena suspected that his son was better to him than what he let on. Especially considering the amount of espresso beans the man brought.

"Do you tell him you give them to me? Or do you let him think you eat them?"

Joe turned his head toward her and looked at her with his bushy brows shielding his face, his blue eyes squinting so much she could barely tell their color. "What do you think?"

"I think that's a smile peeking around your mouth. Be careful, because I'm going to start to think that you're just a big old softy and not the crusty old man you want everybody to believe you are."

"Nobody cares." He huffed, looking back out toward the lake.

"That's why I'm here. Because I don't care."

"You're here for the espresso beans."

"You know, sometimes I feel like no one cares about me either."

She didn't usually talk about serious subjects with him. Typically, she tried to tease him out of his bad mood. More and more, he had to hide his face to keep a smile from showing.

It always made her feel good when she felt like she left him in a better mood than what he was when she found him. Personally, she thought he just enjoyed the company. Everyone liked to have someone to talk to occasionally.

As far as she knew, Joe's son and she were the only visitors he had.

"A young chick like you. You got your whole life ahead of you."

She snorted. "You're just as much of a young chick as I am."

"I doubt it," Joe said.

She figured he was probably ten years older than she was. He looked older than what he was because of being out in the elements all his life. From the little they talked, particularly on the Michigan winter afternoons when she managed to walk up the beach, she learned he'd been a commercial fisherman working for one of the big fisheries between Chicago and Milwaukee. It had been a hard life. And he had to be away from his family, at the lighthouse, for weeks at a time.

Then he had a tragedy, losing his wife and two sons, and she suspected that he'd never really gotten over it.

That was part of the reason she'd been so worried about Sunday. Losing a child could destroy a person's life. She only hoped that Sunday would turn to the Lord instead of allowing it to break her.

It looked like Sunday had done that, and Lena figured she probably had Noah to thank.

Noah and Hope.

"My kid suggested that I sell the bed-and-breakfast. I haven't been able to figure out what to do."

"Don't let them take it from you. But if you make enough money, and you use it wisely, you might not have to work again."

"That's just it. It's not that I don't want to work. I do. But it would be nice to have a few more days off than what I currently have. I always have to be there, although I know that Sunday or any of my kids will help me out if I need it."

"Don't be afraid to ask. Sometimes people want to help you but don't know how."

She was surprised hearing those words come out of his mouth. He didn't seem like the kind of man who would say those kinds of things. But sometimes people surprised a person.

They sat in silence for a while, with her not really having words to say, just mulling over the idea in her mind.

She really wanted to sell, but she didn't want to leave her old life. She was afraid of change; she didn't want to upend everything. Didn't want to move out of the house she'd lived in since she got married, give up the business that she'd struggled to run since her husband had walked out on her.

But change wasn't the enemy. Maybe a lack of change was the enemy. Should she walk forward, embracing the newness of her life?

She hadn't gotten anything decided two hours later, when she stood up and bid Joe a good day. He seemed sad to watch her walk away and reminded her to take her fish and her espresso beans.

She didn't want to end up old and bitter. Not that Joe was either of those, just... She wanted to be a blessing to people, not withdraw into herself and have nothing to do with her days except fish and complain.

Was that what would happen to her if she sold the bed-and-breakfast?

Sunday twisted her fingers together and tried to make her lungs work properly. She was finally going to meet Business Boy. She'd actually had to turn down a request from Noah to do something with him this evening when they'd fed Hope together. He'd been fine with it. He'd said he had some things to do as well, and it was for the best.

He'd walked back with her to the bed and breakfast and told her he'd call her.

She'd been hoping he'd kiss her - he'd been gone for almost two weeks and she'd been thinking about kissing him a lot while he wasn't around. Funny that she would have said that she'd never want to do the relationship thing again, but with Noah...he'd changed her mind, anyway.

She should have told him she was meeting someone, but it seemed odd that she didn't have any information about Business Boy and she didn't want Noah to worry. If they were "officially" together, she definitely would have, but since he hadn't even kissed her, hadn't asked for any kind of commitment or given one of his own...well, she didn't want to assume more than she should. Maybe their relationship was just friends and that was the way it would stay. Friends who held hands. A friend who bought a filly for her.

She put her hand on the diner door. Could she see anyone sitting alone with candy in front of them?

Her eyes roved over the tables and booths, finally landing on one where a man sat alone with his back toward her. It had to be Business Boy, unless he wasn't there yet, since it was the only booth or table with a single man sitting at it.

She took a breath and opened the door.

The man's hair was dark, a similar color to Noah's. He wore a button up and his hands sat on the table in front of him, long fingers, short nails and they looked like capable hands. She liked them. They were younger-looking than she expected. Very much like Noah's hands. She'd worked with Noah a good bit with Hope and had always admired his hands.

A flat rectangular box with a blue ribbon on it sat beyond his hands.

The candy.

This was Business Boy.

Sunday swallowed, allowed her lips to turn up and stepped up to the table.

"Hi. I'm-" Her voice cut off mid sentence as she got a good look at the man when he turned his head and looked toward the sound of her voice. "Noah?"

Business Boy was Noah?

His face held a bit of a smile, but concern wrinkled his brow.

Maybe because he knew who she was - he'd started writing to her because of Blake - and he must have been concerned about her reaction to him.

What was her reaction? After surprise, of course. She wasn't upset. He hadn't lied to her in any way, or tried to take advantage of her. He'd just reached out without telling her who he was. Maybe because of their backgrounds.

"Why didn't you tell me?"

"You're not mad?" he asked as he stood to greet her.

"No." She drew the word out, like she had to think about it, making sure it was the right answer. It was. "I guess I see why you didn't say anything at first, but why didn't you later? Especially after we started hanging out more?"

"I guess I wasn't sure how. The longer it took me to figure out how and what to say when I told you, the more concerned I was that I'd ruin anything we started. And I didn't want to lose you again."

"Lose me?" She didn't understand. What did he think was going to happen?

"You chose Glen. I guess I can't lose something I never really had, but I did lose a friend."

"Glenn was a mistake." That was so true. "One I learned a good bit from, and one who helped me become a better person, but still a mistake."

"And I still lost you over him. I didn't want to lose you again."

She blinked. She hadn't realized he thought like that.

"You look surprised."

"I...I." It sounded like, even back in high school, he didn't think of her as a friend. How did she say that?

He waited.

"I thought we were friends. But..."

"I wanted more." His lips flattened. "I always wanted more."

"Always?" She hadn't known.

"Yeah."

They stared at each other. She could read the truth in his gaze. He really had wanted to be more than friends with her. The truth of that was there now.

She touched her tongue to her lip and then decided to try to be brave. "I thought about kissing you a lot while you were gone."

One side of his mouth turned up slowly.

"Tell me more."

Just like that her anxiety was gone and she laughed. "That pretty much says it all, I think."

"I guess it does. You wouldn't be thinking about kissing me if you didn't have some strong feelings for me."

"That's true. I...I missed you. Missed talking with you, being with you, laughing, especially laughing with you."

There was still laughter in his eyes, but there was a different look, something a little deeper, maybe. Something that said her words were the right ones.

"I hoped, hoped you enjoyed being with me half as much as I loved being with you. I didn't want to push. Maybe that was why I kept doing the letters, too. I wanted as much from you as I could get."

That made her heart sigh. That he wanted to be with her so much.

"It was fun to write the letters. They were a big help to me right when I really needed it. The letters, and you." She paused. "I'm ready for more." She didn't say that as confidently as she hoped to.

"Me too. I have been for a while. It would probably shock you if I told you how long

I've wanted to ask if you'd be interested in something more than friends. Building something that would last a lifetime. I want that with you. The thought of not having you with me for the rest of my life isn't one I want to entertain. I've been hoping for so much more."

"I'm interested in more. But I wouldn't mind if we start with kissing."

"Here?" he asked on a laugh before he looked around the diner.

"Anywhere," she said, being honest, her heart galloping.

His eyes glinted, but he put his arms around her and pulled her to him. "Maybe a hello kiss?" he murmured.

"Any kind," she whispered back before their mouths met and she forgot about the diner and the people around them and just settled into Noah's arms, which felt like the most perfect place she'd ever been. They felt like home and she never wanted to leave.

After they ate, they got Hope, whom Sunday had been teaching to lead, and they walked, hand in hand, along the beach enjoying the sunset and each other.

They didn't know whether Lena would sell the bed and breakfast or how things with the hotel would turn out, but one thing they did know, whatever happened, they wanted to do it together. And that filled her with hope. Hope for a

beautiful future, side by side, with someone who had loved her for a long time
and who wanted to love her forever.

Maybe they didn't do as much walking as
they did holding hands and kissing, but
Sunday told Noah later it was the most
romantic day of her life.

Eleanor Landry braided the ribbon into Hope's mane. Eleanor usually worked on dogs, but since she was the only place in Strawberry Sands that was even close to being able to handle a horse and get it all dolled up to be in a wedding, she'd volunteered to help her sister Sunday get her filly ready for the big day.

Even more crazily, she'd agreed to help the ladies of Strawberry Sands put on their first ever Christmas Barn Dance in December. What did she know about organizing and planning a barn dance? She didn't even know how to dance, let alone how to plan one.

She'd skipped all the high school dances because she just couldn't see how it would be any fun. Animals had always been her thing and spending an evening around kids who were sweating, jumping and screaming to be heard over the music didn't sound like a fun time to her.

But the folks wanted a barn dance, and she seemed to be one of the only people in town who wasn't newly married and had time to work on the planning and the execution.

She stood back to admire her handiwork as Hope stretched her head around and tried to eat one of the ribbons.

"I know it kind of looks like grass, but it's not edible and will give you a belly ache. Not recommended." She scratched Hope's neck, which was soft and silky and warm.

Wanting to bury her head in the clean fur, she resisted, since she'd spent an hour at the new hairdresser in town getting her hair and makeup just right. She didn't want to ruin anything.

"Don't be nervous. You're going to do just fine," she murmured to the horse, but she was really talking to herself. Doing the people thing was not something she was comfortable with. She was much happier in her doggie salon, handling her four-legged customers. Dogs she understood. People? Not so much.

Maybe that was why she was unmarried.

Probably some. But she'd also had a boyfriend from tenth grade through her sophomore year of college when she'd found out he'd been cheating on her almost from day one of their relationship. If she could spend six years with someone and not know he wasn't being faithful the entire time, she really had no business trying again. Not that she even wanted to. She'd felt - and still did - like the biggest idiot in the entire world.

Dogs were better than men any day.

That's what she told herself as she stood with her sister while Sunday said her vows and the preacher pronounced her and Noah man and wife and Noah kissed his new bride.

The day was perfect, the ceremony beautiful, and her sister glowed in a way that didn't happen when a person loved a dog. Eleanor stifled her snort just in time.

Yeah, maybe she'd love to find someone who looked at her the way Noah looked at Sunday, but most of her said that the potential pain wasn't worth the risk.

She'd stick with dogs and being behind the scenes at barn dances. That was safer.

Enjoy this preview of There I Find Light, just for you!

Chapter 1

"Who is the dude standing over there in the corner?" Norma Jean asked Eleanor Landry as they stood by the punch bowl at the first annual Strawberry Sands Christmas barn dance.

Eleanor glanced over the rim of her cup. "That's Peter Slessing. He's the brother of the business partner of my sister's husband, Noah."

"Oh my goodness, you're related to him?" Norma Jean said with her mouth hanging wide open.

Maybe that was a little confusing. She could understand how Norma Jean didn't quite get it. But she didn't know how else to explain him, because Peter wasn't exactly a part of Strawberry Sands.

"He just bought a farm outside of town this year. So, he's kind of new around town."

"I thought you said he was related to you?" Norma Jean slanted him another glance out of the corner of her eye.

Eleanor knew what that look meant a mile away. Norma Jean was interested in the handsome farmer.

Eleanor could understand why. The man was attractive, with his square jaw, the dark stubble on his cheeks, and the cowboy hat that sat low on his forehead. Of course, he was wearing a button-down plaid shirt along with jeans and boots. Eleanor was a sucker for boots.

But Norma Jean was interested, and Eleanor wouldn't have anything to do with a man who someone else had already declared as a love interest, especially when that someone was the cousin of her best friend, Sally.

"He doesn't seem to want to date any of the girls in town though," Eleanor said, wanting Norma Jean to be informed.

"Is this the guy that you were telling me wasn't interested in anyone?"

"Yeah. Different people have approached him, and he's just been kinda standoffish." She was going to stop there, but she thought maybe she should give the man the benefit of the doubt. "My mom says he's just busy getting his farm ready for winter, but…" She looked around the barn. She had been in charge of making sure it was decorated for Christmas, with wreaths hanging up on the doors, twinkle lights hanging from the rafters, and festive ribbons and bows everywhere, along with four different Christmas trees, complete with presents underneath them. Christmas music played out of portable speakers, and there was a jovial, happy atmosphere. She had to say she was pleased with her handiwork.

"Winter has more than descended," she said.

"Maybe I can figure out how to get him to be less standoffish." Norma Jean wiggled her brows.

"Good luck with that. I'm surprised he's even here. Probably Franklin dragged him along with him."

"Franklin?"

"He's a businessman from Chicago and partner to my sister's husband."

"Oh. That's how the family connection comes in."

"Yeah, a connection, but no relation." Eleanor hadn't spent too much time getting to know Franklin. He'd been around, and she knew him to recognize him, but he always seemed preoccupied with whatever it was that he did in Chicago.

Her sister Sunday indicated that he might be moving to Strawberry Sands and in fact had bought property along with Noah, her husband. But Franklin didn't seem as interested in moving to a small town.

Eleanor allowed her eyes to drift over the crowd until she found Franklin standing in the corner. He had been talking to Noah earlier, but she saw Noah following along behind his wife as she led him to the dance floor.

Now Franklin stood by himself, his head down, scrolling on his phone. She got the feeling that he would rather be anywhere other than where he was.

"I'm going to go ask him to dance," Norma Jean said, draining the last of her punch and setting her cup down at the end of one of the picnic tables set up by the refreshment table. "Wish me luck."

Eleanor couldn't get any words out before Norma Jean walked away. She wanted to tell her to come back. For some reason, neither Franklin nor Peter seemed like the marrying type. Or interested in a small-town girl type. Maybe that was more what she meant.

But then, Norma Jean wasn't the kind of person who sat back and allowed life to happen to her. Unlike Eleanor.

Eleanor shifted, not liking the direction her thoughts were going. She didn't want to be the kind of person who life happened to. She wanted to be the kind of person who grabbed life by the horns and fitted it to suit her.

Well, she wanted to do the Lord's will too. But she didn't think God wanted her sitting in a corner, wishing her life was different, rather than going out and making it different.

If you were going to do that, you'd walk over there and ask Franklin to dance with you.

That was true. But she didn't want to. He might say no.

And what's going to happen to you if he says no?

Good question. Nothing. Other than she'd be embarrassed, and the next few times she saw him at any kind of town or family get-together, she'd want to hide in a corner.

Why? What's so terrible about asking someone to dance, having them decline? It doesn't mean anything. You simply found out they weren't interested. It's not like you're going to risk your life or anything.

She didn't like the little voice in her head. Well, she appreciated it, because it was trying to get her out of her corner and into a more active lifestyle.

She knew her mother worried about her, and Eleanor hated to add that extra burden to her. Her mom had been so good to her, and she wanted to return the favor. She knew there were a lot of people who turned their backs on their parents as they got older or, at the very least, shut their parents out of their lives and didn't give them any say in it. She couldn't see any justification for that in the Bible, and indeed, the Bible taught that a child should listen to their parents and absorb the wisdom that was shared. After all, who loved a person more than their mother?

Her mother only wanted the best for her.

But she didn't want to take the risk of rejection.

If you don't change something, you can't expect anything to change.

She wasn't sure exactly what that meant, although it kind of made sense in her head. She couldn't expect her life to go in a different direction if she wasn't willing to do anything different to make it change direction.

All right.

She glanced across the room. Norma Jean had gotten waylaid by Miss Heather. Miss Heather could be quite a force of nature, and as Eleanor watched, Norma Jean started to walk away, but Miss Heather grabbed her arm, pulling her back and continuing to talk.

If you move fast, you could be dancing with Franklin before Norma Jean even gets to Peter.

Eleanor wasn't typically a competitive person, but if she was turning over a new leaf, she might as well turn it over all the way.

Taking her cup and setting it down on the picnic table beside Norma Jean's, she took a breath and decided that she would do something totally out of character. She would walk over to Franklin and ask him to dance.

The barn felt a lot bigger when she was standing on the other side of it, but the walk across seemed short. She found herself praying that Miss Heather would let Norma Jean go and come over and waylay her.

That's silly. You can do this. You're an adult.

Maybe this was why she worked as a dog groomer. She could relate to dogs.

They were easy. Hard to offend, pretty happy with anything, and food motivated them.

Unlike people. Who usually weren't happy with anything, were easy to offend—Eleanor seemed to stick her foot in her mouth more times than not—and she still hadn't figured out what motivated most people.

Maybe it was because she'd been rejected so much when she was younger. She just seemed awkward in conversations, always saying something that no one else understood. Her mind went in different directions, while everyone else in the room seemed to be thinking on the same wavelength.

She'd kind of given up ever fitting in anywhere. Which was why she was alone, a dog groomer, and not married like her siblings. Ryan was the only other one who hadn't gotten married, and she could understand why. He'd been busy on the rodeo circuit, going from place to place, never staying in one spot very long. He hadn't had time to settle down.

But now that he was back in Strawberry Sands to stay, she was sure he'd be married before the end of next year.

But her. She was pretty much hopeless. Except, she was turning over that new leaf. It was practically spinning since she was going to go over and ask Franklin to dance. He would say yes, and they would have an engaging conversation while they danced without stepping on each other's toes to a whole big pile of Christmas songs that would become their new playlist after they got married two Christmases from now.

Yeah, and if Franklin had any idea what she was thinking, he would run in the opposite direction as she walked toward him.

She should just take it moment by moment. Live in the moment. Wasn't that the advice that everyone was given?

She'd never been able to do that either. She had her whole life planned out. Of course, nothing had gone as planned, especially after her longtime high school boyfriend, who also happened to be her boyfriend through two years of college, had broken up with her.

And it wasn't just that he had broken up with her; after he walked away, she found out from different people that he'd been cheating on her the entire time they'd been together.

She felt like an idiot. And at the time, she vowed never to have another relationship. But that seemed like a stupid thing to do, she just...hadn't been able to get back in the game. Or maybe she hadn't developed the skills necessary to play the game.

Or maybe there wasn't a game. After all, dating wasn't really necessary, was it? It was a modern thing. Two hundred years ago, people didn't date. Which she could really appreciate at this point in her life.

And with that thought, she was standing in front of Franklin, who didn't look up from his phone.

"Excuse me," Eleanor said, trying to swallow her nervousness, although she couldn't keep from twisting her hands together in front of her.

Franklin finished the text or whatever he was doing before he looked up. He looked around, his eyes widening before they landed back on her.

Franklin might not ever grace the cover of a modeling magazine, and he most likely wouldn't land on bodybuilders.com, but his dark hair was neatly clipped, and his eyes were a rich, deep brown behind the glasses that perched on his nose.

They must be for reading, because he looked at her over them.

"Are you talking to me?" he asked, like she wasn't standing directly in front of him.

"Dance me with you like I mean would." The words came out of her mouth, but even she was confused about what she was trying to say. So it was no surprise when Franklin's brows drew down.

"Again, please? This time in English?"

She wanted to fall through the floor. Had she ever been more embarrassed in her entire life? Probably. She'd done lots of embarrassing things. But she was having trouble remembering anything that was quite this bad.

She needed to apologize for being so confusing.

"My sorry bad dancer you few." That didn't come out right either. Apparently, she combined asking him to dance again with apologizing for messing up her first invitation.

Her brain never could do two things at once, and apparently her mouth was even worse at it.

She was opening her mouth to try to make some sense out of the situation, as Franklin seemed to be genuinely interested in what she was trying to say, or maybe he was just concerned that the insane asylum had had a breakout, when his phone buzzed loudly.

He glanced down, looked at the phone screen for a moment, then looked back up. "I'm sorry. I have to take this."

He swiped on his phone, put it to his ear, and said, "Hello?" as he turned and walked a few steps away from her. Considering they were standing in a corner, he couldn't get far, but that was all it took.

Eleanor considered herself the most inept person in the world, put her tail between her legs, and scurried away.

You can continue reading by getting
There I Find Light.

newsletter – I laughed so hard I sprayed it out all over the table!"

Claim your free book from Jessie!